FRIENDSHIP BLOOMS IN HONEY GROVE

A BRAXTON FAMILY ROMANCE BOOK 2

ANNE-MARIE MEYER

To my family

Join my Newsletter!

Find great deals on my books and other sweet romance!

Get, Fighting Love for the Cowboy FREE

just for signing up!

Grab it HERE!

She's an IRS auditor desperate to prove herself.

He's a cowboy trying to hold onto his ranch.

Love was not on the agenda.

CHAPTER ONE

The roaring sound of Jonathan's Jaguar faded into the night as he pulled into his parents' driveway and killed the engine. After taking a deep breath, he glanced out the windshield and up at the familiar white house with red shutters and a porch that wrapped all the way around.

Well, not much had changed here.

And really, that was true of all of Honey Grove, SC.

It never changed.

Even shirtless Dan was still wandering the streets of the neighborhood. Jonathan had passed by him as he drove to his parent's house. He was harmless, but age hadn't done him any favors with his gut spilling over the top of his pants.

Dan waved his walking stick as he walked behind Jonathan's car, tapping the trunk with his hand.

Jonathan lifted his hand and gave him a small wave.

"Welcome home, Jonny!" Dan said in his familiar, gravely voice.

"Yep," Jonathan said, wincing at the nickname he'd grown up with. Then he sighed.

Welcome home.

He was back.

He slipped his keys from his ignition and got out. After slamming the door, he went to the trunk and grabbed his duffel bag.

It was going to be nice to spend a few months at home. July was his off-season, and after hanging out in Atlanta for a while with his friend Zach, Jonathan was ready to come home. Things in his life were rocky, and some familiarity would do him some good.

He threw his keys into the air as he passed by his oldest brother's truck. He tapped the truck's body, excitement brewing in his stomach. It'd been a long time since he'd seen his brother Josh and his nephew, Jordan. Josh recently returned home to Honey Grove after a messy divorce that left him with nothing except his five-year-old son and a broken heart.

Jonathan jogged up the back-porch steps and tried the door handle. To his relief, the door was open. He turned the handle and stepped into the kitchen that he'd grown up in. The familiar smell of cookies lingered in the air. Smiling, Jonathan shut the door behind him and slipped his duffel bag from his shoulder to the floor. He made his way to the Snoopy cookie jar that his mom kept on the counter. It was faded from years of use, but it was a staple in the Braxton household. If his mom ever got rid of it, she'd have a mutiny on her hands.

The lid clinked as he returned it to the jar.

"I should have known it was you," Sondra Braxton said as she emerged from the hallway that fed into the kitchen. She wore a robe, and her greying black hair was pulled up into curlers. The smile on her face hadn't changed. It was still warm and inviting and caused the sides of her eyes to crinkle.

"Ma," Jonathan said as he reached out his arms and engulfed her in a hug.

She laughed as she pulled back and squeezed his biceps. "Holy cow, child of mine. These are getting a bit out of hand."

Jonathan dropped his arms and felt his muscles. "They are not. I work hard on these babies."

Sondra raised her eyebrows. "They're almost as big as your head."

Jonathan shrugged as he shoved a cookie into his mouth and then grabbed six more.

"Slow down," his mom chided. "You'll get sick."

Jonathan ignored her and made his way to the cupboard to find a cup. Then he grabbed the milk jug from the fridge and filled up his glass. After the cookies and milk were demolished, he set the glass down next to the sink, only to hear the tsking of his mom.

"Okay, okay," he said, as he rinsed the cup and stuck it in the dishwasher. He turned, folding his arms across his chest and leaning against the counter. "Some things never change." He gave her a wink.

Sondra was watching him in her normal, prying-mom way. Her eyebrows were raised and her lips pursed.

"What?" Jonathan asked. For some reason, he got the feeling that his mom already knew everything he was trying to hide.

Sondra just shrugged. "How's Zach?"

Jonathan pushed his hands through his hair and shrugged. "He's good. Engaged."

Sondra's eyes widened. "Before you?"

Realizing that he wasn't going to get through a single conversation with his mom without her bringing up the fact that all of her children were still single, he sighed and grabbed his duffel bag. "It's not a competition, Ma."

Sondra snorted and followed him up the stairs. "It's not

now. He's got you beat. I thought you two were always competing. How can you let him win at this?"

Jonathan let out a loud groan, hoping his mom would pick up on his tone. But from the expectant look on her face, she didn't. Or, if she did, she didn't care. She stepped in front of him with her arms folded.

"I want more grandbabies," she said, her voice low and threatening.

Jonathan stopped and stared down at her. It was comical that she thought he would be intimidated by her when she stood barely five-foot three. But her small stature didn't change the look in her eye, and, in that moment, he felt like a little kid staring up at his mom again.

He'd been on the receiving end of her wrath a few times as a kid. He knew what lurked beneath her sweet smile. "You've got four other kids to help you with that."

Sondra sighed, blowing a piece of graying hair from her face. "Trust me, the next time I see them, I'm going to let them know. Josh is living in the apartment above the garage, and I've already got plans for him."

Jonathan dipped down and gave her a quick kiss on the top of her head. He needed to stop this before she could continue. "Love you, Mom, but I'm beat. Can we pick up this conversation tomorrow?"

Sondra studied him and then nodded, reaching up to pat him on the cheek. "I only say these things because I love you. I don't want any of my babies to be alone."

A strange, yet all too familiar feeling rose up in Jonathan's throat as his mom's words settled around him. Truth was, he'd been feeling more and more alone lately. Especially when it seemed like everyone around him had someone.

Why couldn't he find that one girl? The one who set his heart and soul on fire?

Not wanting to break down in front of him mom,

Jonathan just smiled and headed toward the stairs. "I'll see you in the morning," he called over his shoulder.

"Dad's got things set up at the site for you. He'll be waking you up early."

"Okay," Jonathan shouted as he walked down the hallway toward his old bedroom.

After shoving his clothes into the dresser drawers, he climbed into his bed and pulled the covers over his shoulder. He let out his breath as he sunk into the old mattress.

It felt good to be home. He was ready for a change, and coming back to the beginning felt like the perfect place to start over.

"Get up."

Jonathan jolted up from the dead of sleep to find his dad hovering over him. Jimmy wasn't a slight man, and, even though his skin had wrinkled more and his hair had thinned, he was still the formidable man that Jonathan remembered as a kid.

A smile broke out over his face. "Hey, Dad," he said.

Jimmy grunted. "Shower and come downstairs. We don't want to be late."

Jonathan yawned and pulled off the covers. With both feet firmly planted on the ground, he rubbed his face, hoping it would wake him up. "I'm up. I'll be down in a minute."

After a quick shower, he dried off and dressed in a t-shirt and jeans. Once he slipped on his socks, he made his way downstairs to find his mom had made a gigantic breakfast.

"Really, Ma? Who are you expecting this morning? An army?"

Sondra shot him a look as she raised her spatula in the

air. "Hey, sometimes old habits die hard. Besides, last time we had you in the house, you were bulking up."

Jimmy was sitting at the table, drinking his coffee and reading the paper. "Bulking up, woman?" he asked, peeking at Jonathan over his readers. "If Jonathan bulked up any more, he'd burst."

Jonathan chuckled as he filled a mug of coffee and joined his dad. Just as his butt hit the seat, Sondra appeared with a plate full of eggs, bacon, and pancakes.

"Mom—" Jonathan started, only to have his mom shush him.

"You need to keep up your strength. How would the team feel if you let yourself go on the off-season?" she asked as she drizzled his pancakes with syrup. Like he was a kid at risk of spilling all over the table if left to do it alone.

"Let the boy serve himself, Sondra," Jimmy said in his gruff voice full of affection.

Sondra handed over a fork, completely ignoring him. "It's fine. I'm just helping."

Jimmy scoffed as he turned back to his paper. "Were you just 'helping' Josh when you suggested that Beth nanny for him?"

Jonathan was mid-chew when his dad's words settled in around him. "Beth's back?" He'd graduated high school with her and Tiffany. They'd been like the three musketeers.

Jimmy nodded and let the corner of his newspaper fall. "Yes. But your mother's got a plan."

Sondra reached over and swatted Jimmy with a hand towel. "Don't go spoiling it now, or all my hard work will be for nothing."

Jimmy just chuckled as he straightened the paper and focused back on whatever article he was reading.

"Well, I'm good, Mom. Do what you want with Josh, but I'm not really interested in finding anyone right now."

"I know," Sondra sang out in her *I'm listening, but not really* voice.

Jonathan decided it was better to focus on his food than to argue with his mom about his love life. Nothing good ever came of that.

Once breakfast was finished, Jimmy announced that it was time to go. Jonathan slipped on his work boots and headed out the door behind his dad. After climbing into the truck, Jimmy pulled out of the driveway.

The fifteen-minute drive to Braxton Construction brought back so many memories. Honey Grove was starting to update the city, but it was slow going, which Jonathan was almost grateful for. It was nice to know that he could come back to his childhood town and everything would basically be the same.

Jimmy pulled into the gravel parking lot of their building and killed the engine. Jonathan noticed that Josh's truck was parked on the far end of the lot. He pulled open his door and climbed out. He was excited to see his brother again. It had really been too long since they last spoke.

Jonathan followed after his dad as they walked to the front door of their building. Cool air hit Jonathan as he entered.

A very familiar squeal sounded from the front desk, and Tiffany appeared right in front of him. She wrapped her arms around him and leapt up, knowing he'd catch her.

"You're finally back," she exclaimed—right in his ear.

Jonathan pulled her into a huge bear hug and spun her around. Then he set her down and stuck his finger in his ear as he winced. "Geez, Tiff. Trying to deafen me?"

Tiffany giggled as she swatted his arm. "It was not that loud." Then her expression stilled. "I can't believe you're back."

Jonathan shoved his hands into his front pockets and shrugged. "It was about time."

Her dark brown eyes danced with enthusiasm as she nodded. "Yeah, it was. It's been too long since I last saw you. It's hard to be Leia when I don't have my Luke."

Jonathan winced. They'd been obsessed with Star Wars growing up. "Don't remind me," he said.

Tiffany's face fell. "Wait a minute. You're telling me that I bought these for nothing?" She disappeared behind her desk and emerged with two lightsabers.

"Oh, man. Seriously?" Jonathan held out his hand for the blue one. "Well, it wasn't a total mistake," he said as he steadied his stance.

"It's on." Tiffany lunged forward and began to make the humming sound from the movies.

It wasn't until Jonathan had Tiffany pinned against the wall that Josh came walking out of Jimmy's office. His eyebrows rose as his gaze landed on them.

"Fighting again?" Josh asked, distracting Jonathan from his victory and allowing Tiffany to slip through his grasp and stab the lightsaber into his back.

"You're dead," Tiffany called out.

Jonathan made some dying noises as he collapsed on the ground. "You distracted me," he said, shooting a fake angry look at Josh.

Josh just shook his head. "You two are dorks."

Jonathan popped up and rushed over to his brother to give him a hug. After they embraced, Josh pulled back and tousled Jonathan's hair.

"Even though you're built like a tank now, it doesn't mean that I can't whip your butt."

Jonathan chuckled. "I'd like to see you try."

Josh flexed his muscles and then shook his head. "I would, but I don't think that the Steeler's want their star player getting schooled by his older brother." Josh reached out and patted Jonathan's shoulder. "It's for your dignity, man."

Jonathan shook his head as Josh said goodbye to Tiffany and headed out the door. Jimmy emerged from his office with keys to a company truck and a list of things that Jonathan needed to do. After giving him a few brief instructions, Jimmy left to head to the Young remodel, leaving Jonathan and Tiffany alone.

Jonathan glanced over at Tiffany, who had settled into her chair behind the desk. Her hair was longer now, falling in thick curls down her back. She tucked a strand behind her ear as she stared at the computer screen in front of her.

Being around Tiffany calmed him. Even though he wasn't sure where his life was going, seeing her settled him down. She made it seem okay that his future was a dark room with no lights. Or the fact that he had no answers to the questions plaguing his mind. A smile played on his lips.

Tiffany must have noticed because she glanced up and her cheeks flushed. "What are you staring at?" she asked as she rubbed her nose.

Jonathan shrugged. "Nothing. It's just good to be home."

Tiffany leaned forward on her elbows and nodded. "It's good to have you back." Her smile was genuine and familiar.

Feeling a little ridiculous just standing there and expressing his feeling to her, Jonathan lifted the to-do list and tapped it. "I should get started on this, or Dad will have my head."

Tiffany nodded as she began clicking keys on the keyboard again. "Meet me at the Tavern tonight? I'm sure Sean will want to say hi."

Jonathan was on his way to the door but stopped when he heard Sean's name. "You're dating that tool again? How many guys does that make for you? Fifteen?"

Tiffany's fingers stopped moving, and her once warm

gaze had turned stormy. "It has not been that many guys, And, besides, Sean is not a tool. Don't tell me that you're still holding a grudge. That was years ago."

Jonathan cleared his throat as frustration rose up inside of him. "He almost broke my leg, Tiff. It would have ruined my career." Why was she defending a guy she just started seeing? He had years as Tiffany's friend, she should be loyal to *him*, not guy number 15.

Tiffany was leaning back in her chair with her arms folded. "But he didn't, and now you're the star football player and he's not." She leaned forward with a begging hint to her gaze. "Can you just move on? Please? For me?"

Jonathan studied her and then sighed. "Fine. I promise to be pleasant."

Tiffany nodded as her smile returned. "Thank you. I don't want to have to pick between my best friend and boyfriend, so if you two could just get along, that would make my life so much easier."

Jonathan dipped into a low bow. "Anything for Princess Leia," he said and then straightened, giving her a wink.

Tiffany sat straighter as she nodded, a sudden royal air about her. "You are dismissed, my loyal subject."

Jonathan smiled as he pulled open the door and stepped out into the hot South Carolina air. "I'll see you tonight," he said as he pulled the door closed and headed out to the truck.

Sure, his dad had just assigned him a bunch of busywork, but it took his mind off the stress in his life, and he was grateful for that.

CHAPTER TWO

Tiffany twisted on the bar stool at the Tavern. She was sitting next to a very irritated Sean with pinched lips and folded arms. The fact that Jonathan was joining them for drinks had him in a foul mood.

So much so that Tiffany's stomach was in knots. Anxiety rose up inside of her as she kept flicking her gaze over to the door, not sure what she was going to do when Jonathan came walking in.

"I just don't understand why he has to join us," Sean said as he unfolded his arms and grabbed the beer in front of him. He took a long pull and then set it down.

"Sean, we've been over this. He's my best friend and I haven't seen him in a long time. Come on, can't you just put the past behind you?" Tiffany reached out and wrapped her arms around his waist and pulled herself closer to him.

Sean tensed for a minute and then relaxed, glancing down at her, his expression softening. "You know I have issues with Braxton," he said. His voice was quieter now. Less tense.

Tiffany nodded as if she understood, but she really didn't. Both guys were acting ridiculous. It'd been so long ago that it was a little childish that they were acting this way, but she couldn't tell them that. It was best to just have them hang out together so that they could see how stupid they were acting.

Sean wrapped his arms around Tiffany and pulled her close, dipping down to press his lips against hers. Relief flooded her body as she kissed him back. Defusing Sean had become an art that she'd perfected. He was a good guy; he just got frustrated a bit too easily—especially when it came to Jonathan Braxton.

A huge cheer sounded in the bar, causing Sean to pull away and glance over toward the door. Tiffany's heart picked up speed and Sean's whole body tensed as Jonathan entered the Tavern. A flurry of moving bodies pushed past them and over to where Jonathan stood. Most of the room was either taking turns shaking his hand or clapping him on the back.

"Typical," Sean said as he turned back to the bar and downed his beer.

All the hope that had risen in Tiffany's chest deflated as she watched Sean's shoulders tighten when Jonathan walked up.

"Hey, Tiff," Jonathan said, reaching his arm around her and giving her a quick peck on the top of her head.

She whipped her gaze around and stared at Jonathan, hoping he'd get the hint.

He furrowed his brow as he stared at her. She held his gaze and then tipped her head toward Sean, who was spinning his now empty bottle on the counter.

Jonathan looked confused, but then realization dawned on him. He leaned forward and clapped his hand on Sean's shoulder. "Hey, man, it's good to see you."

Tiffany hoped that Sean might actually be nice, but that disappeared when she saw Sean's jaw flex and his gaze harden. He turned to Jonathan, breaking the contact between them.

"Hey," Sean said, his voice strained.

Jonathan widened his eyes and flicked his gaze over to Tiffany. She softened her gaze, hoping he wouldn't get upset. These were the two most important guys in her life. There was no way she could pick between them. They needed to figure out how to bridge this gap.

Jonathan must have picked up on her body language because he stuck his hand out and smiled at Sean. "I'm good with putting the past behind us if you are," he said.

Sean glanced down at Jonathan's hand and then turned to wave down Freddy and order another beer. When it became apparent that Sean wasn't going to shake Jonathan's hand, Jonathan dropped it, shoving both hands into the front pockets of his jeans.

Once Freddy delivered the beer, Sean grabbed it and then turned to Tiffany. "I can't, Tiff. I'm going to play some darts. You can join me if you want to."

Anger and frustration boiled up inside of her as she stared at Sean. Why was he acting this way? What had happened in high school wasn't that hard to get over. Sure, the scouts had picked Jonathan instead of Sean, but she was sure that enough time had passed for him to get over that. Right?

Sean stormed over to the back of the Tavern, and Tiffany's gaze followed him as he went.

"Well, that was amazing," Jonathan said as he settled onto the stool that Sean had just vacated.

Tiffany sighed and turned to him. "Lay off, Jonathan. He's going through something."

Jonathan met her gaze, dropping his hand in an exaggerated movement. "May I remind you that I haven't done anything wrong?"

Tiffany groaned as she grabbed her Sprite and slipped off

her stool. "Neither have I, and yet I'm the one being punished for this."

Jonathan studied her, and then his expression softened. "I'm sorry. I was a jerk in high school, and I'm sure I could have handled the situation better."

Tiffany sighed, blowing a few loose strands of hair from her face. "You think?"

Jonathan's shoulders slumped. "It's not all it's cracked up to be," he mumbled as he picked up his beer and took a drink.

Confused, Tiffany glanced over at him. "What?"

Jonathan pursed his lips. "Never mind."

Realizing the longer she stood there talking to Jonathan, the madder Sean was going to get, she rested her hand on Jonathan's forearm. "I want to hear about it, but not right now. I've got to go save my relationship."

Jonathan nodded. "I get it. Go. I'll be here."

She gave his arm a squeeze and then made her way back to where Sean was whipping darts at the board. She had to jump out of the way as one went whizzing past her.

Frustrated that Sean was behaving this way, Tiffany stomped up to him and grabbed his arm, halting any further dart throwing.

"What happened to being nice?" she asked.

Sean's face was red with fury as he dropped his arm and began spinning the dart around in his fingers. "I can't do it, Tiff. I just can't. That guy stole my dreams from me. How am I supposed to play nice with him?"

Tiffany tried not to groan. This had to end. "He didn't steal your dreams from you. He just got picked. It happens sometimes. You have to stop blaming Jonathan for everything that went wrong in your life."

Sean glanced over at her, his eyes wide. She could see the anger that resided there. It didn't matter what she said to him, he was going to be angry with Jonathan forever.

"I can't believe you are defending him," Sean said. "It's because of him that I'm stuck in this hellhole. I deserved to get picked over him. I was the better player. Now I'm rotting away in this town with nothing." He stepped past her and flung another dart toward the board.

His words stung as they washed over Tiffany. *Stuck here with nothing*. Was that all she was to him? Nothing?

Unsure of what to say, she folded her arms and glared at him. Part of her wanted to walk away. To let him cool down. But the other part of her—the one that was winning right now—wanted her to stay and fight. She was tired of people making excuses to leave her. Her mom did that. Then her dad. When was she going to find a guy that wasn't going to run at the first sign of struggle?

As if sensing her frustration, Sean turned to study her. Her expression must have said everything because he sighed as he lowered his arm. "Listen, I know he's your friend. But one of these days, you're going to have to pick. Jonathan or me." He pushed his hands through his hair. "If we are going to be anything, I need to be more important to you than an old high school friend." He met her gaze and held it.

Tears formed in her eyes as she studied him. Was he seriously asking her to choose? That wasn't fair. Where did he get the right?

"Don't do this," she whispered as she reached up and angrily flung a tear from her cheek.

Sean's expression softened as he stepped closer to her. "Don't make me. If you want to see where this is going to go. Stay."

Tiffany pinched her lips together as she glanced toward the ceiling, trying to figure out what she was going to do. There's no way she would let Sean dictate who her friends could be. Maybe it was a good idea for them to take a break.

"I can't. Jonathan's my best friend."

Sean studied her for a moment, and then his jaw set as he shrugged. "Then I guess you made your choice." He turned and flung another dart at the board. This one hit sideways, ricocheting off the wall and falling to the floor.

Sean grabbed his beer, gave Tiffany one last look, and shrugged as he walked away.

Frustration and pain built up in her chest as she watched him leave. Part of her wanted to call him back. To convince him that she could still be friends with Jonathan and date him. They could find a way to make this work. But she knew deep inside that wasn't the case. Things between her and Sean were over. At least, for now.

Maybe if he came to his senses, then she'd take him back. But right now, he didn't deserve her. She couldn't let her life be dictated by someone like Sean. If she were that easy to walk away from, maybe they never had what she so desperately believed they did.

Tiffany let out a frustrated sigh as she moved away from the dartboard and weaved through the crowd in search of Jonathan.

She found him leaning against the bar, talking to Spencer. He was friends with Josh and had recently opened up a gym in Honey Grove.

"Sounds like you have some amazing equipment. I'll have to come check it out," Jonathan said as he sipped his beer. Tiffany sidled up next to him, and Jonathan turned and raised his eyebrows as his gaze roamed her face.

Great. He didn't even have to ask to know that something was wrong.

Spencer let out a whoop. "Really? Man, that would be amazing. Having an NFL player work out at my gym would definitely put me on the map."

Jonathan glanced over at Spencer, his once cocky expression faltering. "Ah, man. I doubt that. But I'm happy to help if I can."

Spencer clapped Jonathan on the back and then offered to buy everyone in the bar a round.

Jonathan glanced behind Tiffany. "Where's Sean?"

Tiffany grabbed his beer from his hand and took a drink. "Nope. Off limits. I don't want to talk about that right now.

Jonathan studied her and then leaned forward. "Wanna get out of here?" he asked.

"Yes."

Jonathan laid a twenty down for Freddy and then grabbed her hand and pulled her from the Tavern.

Tiffany took a deep breath of salty air as the door closed behind them. She ran her hands through her hair and tipped her face toward the sky. When she lowered her gaze, she glanced over at Jonathan, who was watching her.

Suddenly self-conscious, Tiffany nudged him with her shoulder. "What?"

Jonathan chuckled. "Nothing."

The crunching of the gravel under their shoes sounded as they walked over to Jonathan's Jaguar.

"Seriously?" Tiffany asked as she walked over and peered into the car. "Flashy much?"

Jonathan chuckled as he shook his head. "Hey, now. It's what all the football players are driving."

Tiffany shot him a look as she nodded. "Sure. Right."

Jonathan threw his keys in the air. "Wanna go for a ride?"

"Um, do you even have to ask?" she teased. She pulled on the door handle and slipped onto the dark leather seat.

Jonathan got in and started the engine, which roared to life. They buckled up, and then Jonathan peeled out of the parking lot and took off down the street.

"Where do you want to go?" he asked.

Tiffany sighed as she stared out the window. There was

so much weight in that question, if only Jonathan knew. "Away from here," she whispered.

"What?" he asked, leaning toward her.

Not wanting to be a downer, she smiled over at him. "The beach."

Jonathan relaxed back in his seat, resting his wrist on the steering wheel. "Perfect."

It took thirty minutes until they were parking in the lot next to their favorite beach. Thankfully, Jonathan had filled the silence with music. Tiffany leaned her head back and belted out the lyrics as the bass thumped around them. One nice thing about having a best friend was you didn't need to talk. Just spending time together was enough.

Jonathan killed the engine and stuffed his key into his pocket as he climbed out.

"Last one to the water is a rotten egg," he yelled as he peeled off down the sand.

"Oh, it's on!" Tiffany yelled as she scrambled to unbuckle and take off after him.

The sound of waves crashing against the shore and the feeling of sand between her toes helped ground her. Tiffany ran, splashing into the water just to have Jonathan grab her around the waist and hoist her up.

"I won!" he yelled as he spun her around.

Tiffany whipped her head back, giggling as she tried not to puke on him. "Jonathan, I'm going to be sick," she exclaimed, hoping he'd pick up on her desperation.

Jonathan chuckled as he set her down. Then he wiggled his eyebrows as he leaned in.

"The island?" he asked.

Tiffany smiled as she nodded. "Of course."

Jonathan reached up and pulled off his shirt. Tiffany balked at how much he'd changed.

As if sensing her stare, Jonathan reached up in an attempt

to cover his pecs. "Don't objectify me," he said, giving her a wink.

"I'm not. It's just hard not to stare. You're like...the Hulk," Tiffany said as she reached out and poked his bicep.

Jonathan flexed it. "Yeah, well, I have to be. If not, I'd get completely run over," he said as he unbuttoned his pants and pulled them off.

He then ran off to the water and dove in.

Tiffany watched him as she stripped down to her underwear. A weird feeling rose up in her stomach as she splashed into the water and began to swim toward Jonathan's bobbing head. They weren't kids anymore, running away together to escape her dad.

Jonathan had been there when everyone decided to leave. When her parents called quits on their marriage and walked off as if their new lives were more important than the broken one they left in Honey Grove. Their broken daughter.

Flipping onto her back and staring up at the star-filled sky, Tiffany took a moment to calm her mind.

This was Jonathan she was thinking about. Jonathan. The guy she'd done a blood oath with as a kid to always stay friends.

Nothing was going to come between them. Nothing.

CHAPTER THREE

Jonathan sprawled out onto the beach as he waited for Tiffany to join him. The secluded island they'd found when they were kids was their hideout. The place they went to get away from the world. It felt great to get back to it. It reminded him of a simpler time, and right now, he needed that in his life.

Splashing drew his attention, and he leaned back on his elbow to watch as Tiffany walked up the beach.

Even though she was his best friend, he found himself appreciating the way her white skin glowed against her black underwear. Something he never would have thought as a kid—and even now, it was a tad strange.

Tiffany must have caught him staring because she hunched over as if to protect herself. "Hey now," she said as she shuffled over and collapsed next to him.

Jonathan pulled up his knees and rested his elbows on them. "You gave *me* a hard time; it's only fair," he said, glancing over at her and giving her a wink.

It may have been his imagination, but Jonathan swore he saw her face flush.

"Yeah, well my transformation isn't as impressive as yours." She reached out to drag her finger through the sand.

Jonathan shrugged. "I wouldn't say that."

Tiffany whipped her gaze up to meet his. "Hey," she said, reaching out to shove his shoulder.

Jonathan chuckled. "I can say this because I'm your best friend, but you're a babe."

Tiffany rolled her eyes. "You're only saying that because I *am* your best friend."

"Okay, fine." Jonathan smiled. Even though he was joking, there was some truth to his words. Tiffany was beautiful. Her dark curly hair covered her shoulders and arms as she held onto her knees. Her dark eyes were wide and soulful. She was amazing.

And Sean was an idiot.

"Are you going to tell me what happened with Sean?" Jonathan asked. For some reason, he had this desire to drive back to the Tavern and punch the guy. Sean had always been a jerk, dragging Tiffany along in their on-again, off-again relationship. Last he knew, they were officially off, never to be on again. Some things never change.

Tiffany sighed as she grabbed a seashell and fiddled with it. "He told me to pick between you two."

Yep. Tool. Man, Jonathan hated that guy. "Really? Wow, what a—"

Tiffany peeked over at him, causing him to pinch his lips shut. He should stop while he was ahead.

"You deserve better," he said, reaching out and placing a sandy hand on her shoulder.

Tiffany leaned toward him, and out of instinct, he wrapped his arm around her shoulders. She leaned her head on his chest, and from the shaking of her shoulders, he could tell she was crying.

"Hey, hey," he said, shifting away so he could catch her

eye. When she didn't look up, he pressed his finger under her chin. Finally, she met his gaze. There was so much hurt there that Jonathan was finding it hard to control his anger.

"Sean is an idiot if he thinks he can find someone better than you. You are…everything." He gave her a smile he hoped told her that he meant what he said.

Tiffany chewed her lip as she studied him. "You think so?"

Jonathan nodded. "A few days away from you and he's going to come running back." Ugh, those words tasted bitter on his tongue. But she looked as if that was what she needed to hear. Especially when her lips tipped up into a smile.

She wrapped her arms around him. "You really are the best friend a girl could ask for."

Jonathan chuckled as he held her close. "Thanks."

A few seconds later, Tiffany pulled away and wiped at her cheeks. She had a determined expression on her face as she faced him. "Alright, tell me what's going on. You're all moody."

Jonathan dropped his arm and shrugged. "Not much. I guess I just…" He met her gaze. Did he really want his best friend to know how much of a loser he was? There was only so much a blood oath could cover.

"Just work. It's stressing me out."

Tiffany nodded and looked as if she were intently listening. "Why is it stressing you out?"

"I might get traded."

Tiffany glanced up at him. "Really? Oh, Jonathan, I'm sorry."

Jonathan reached out and traced his fingers in the sand. "It happens. I just love the Steelers. I don't want to leave."

"It's just a rumor, right?"

"For now."

Tiffany smiled. "Then I bet it'll blow over. You're the best player they have. I wouldn't stress about it until it's for sure."

If only Tiffany understood, she wouldn't sound so sure. But he didn't want to drag down their conversation, so he just nodded. "Yeah. I'm probably freaking out more than I need to."

Tiffany stood and brushed the sand off. "Should we see if our tree is still standing?"

Ready to move on from the heavy discussion, Jonathan stood and nodded. "Yep."

Thankfully their conversation remained light as they walked through the small stand of trees in the center of the island. After making sure the tree that they'd carved their initials into was still standing, Tiffany slapped Jonathan on the shoulder and took off down to the water, yelling that he was "it."

Smiling, Jonathan jumped into the water and swam as fast as he could through the water and to the other beach. Once he was on the shore, he walked up onto the sand and then turned, looking for Tiffany.

A few waves crashed onto the shore, but Tiffany did not come with them. Confused, Jonathan glanced toward the water, hoping to see Tiffany's head bobbing up and down.

Nothing.

Panic rose up inside of Jonathan as he began pacing the water line, looking for her. Where could she be?

He ran his gaze along the path from where he stood to their island, but he didn't see anything. Focusing his gaze, he strained for movement. Any movement.

Then, out of the corner of his eye, he saw a small splash. It was about five feet off from the direction of the island. Not thinking, he dove into the water and pushed as hard as he could to that spot. When he got there, he straightened as he treaded water. Where was she?

Seeing nothing, he dipped below the surface. Despite the fact that his eyes were stinging, he searched the water below.

Then, in the pale light of the moon shining above, he saw her. His heart pounded as he pushed against the current until he could wrap his arms around her waist.

Kicking hard, he pushed toward the surface until he finally broke through, gasping for air. He flipped Tiffany onto her back, and, with one arm firmly wrapped around her, he pushed through the burning sensation in his legs, arms, and lungs as he swam back to shore.

He was so close to the beach, and he just needed to get there. Then he could collapse.

Just when he was sure that he wouldn't make it, Jonathan felt the ground under his feet. His toes dug into the sand as he dragged his body through the crashing waves. And before his body gave way, he laid Tiffany down as carefully as his rubbery muscles could manage before collapsing next to her.

Taking a second to catch his breath, he pushed himself up and crawled over to her.

"Tiffany," he said as he crouched down next to her, waiting for her chest to rise. When he saw no movement, he pressed his fingers against her throat.

Nothing.

Panic coursed through his veins, giving him the strength to pull himself up until he was kneeling next to her. After tipping her face so that her neck was straight, he opened her mouth and blew into it. After a few chest compressions, he blew again.

Every emotion was rushing through him like an avalanche. She needed to breath. She needed to live. This was his best friend, and he'd let her down. Why were they so competitive that he would just leave her in the ocean like that?

"Come on," he yelled as he continued chest compressions.

Glancing up, he took note of his clothes a bit down the shore. He needed his phone so he could call an ambulance.

But if he left to get it, no one would be here to administer CPR.

Cursing under his breath, he blew into her mouth a few times and then returned to compressions. "Don't go, Tiffany," he yelled, his voice breaking under the emotional strain pulling at his soul.

"I can't be here without you," he whispered as he closed his eyes and said a prayer. To God. To anyone who would listen.

Just as his body was about to give out from the physical and emotional strain, he heard a cough, followed by a whole lot of seawater.

Tipping Tiffany onto her side, he held her as she coughed and vomited up more water. Finally, she calmed and he slowly laid her back down on the beach. Her eyes were wide as she glanced around.

Unable to control himself, Jonathan threw his arms around her and squeezed her to his chest. She winced, and just as quickly as he'd hugged her, he let her go.

"Are you okay?" he asked, dipping down to see into her eyes. Just to make sure there was still life in them.

She shivered and brought her arms up to hug her legs. Realizing that she must be freezing, Jonathan told her he would be right back and then rushed over to their clothes and gathered them up.

He returned, shaking the sand out of her clothes and helping her slide on her shirt. Just as he moved to help her with her pants, Tiffany held up her hands.

"I can get dressed," she said, holding out her shaking hand.

He hesitated, but when she gave him an *are you serious?* look, he forced out his overprotective instincts and handed her the pants. Needing a distraction, Jonathan dressed as well.

As Tiffany pulled her pants up to her thighs, she began to shift as if she were trying to stand. Wanting a job, Jonathan lifted her up and then set her feet gently down on the beach. He held her steady as she wiggled into her jeans and buttoned them.

"We should get you to the hospital," he said, glancing around for their shoes.

Tiffany let out a soft laugh. "Hospital? What are you talking about? I'm fine." She waved to the front of her body.

Jonathan shook his head. "This is not an option. You were under for a while. We're going, and I'm not going to let you push me away. It's my job as your best friend."

Sighing, Tiffany nodded. "Fine."

Thankful that she wasn't going to fight him, he looked for their shoes. They were halfway from where they were standing and his car. Bending down, he swiped her legs with his arm and pulled her up, cradling her next to his chest.

"Jonathan, I can walk," she said, tipping her head back so she could stare at him.

There was no way he was going to do that. "No. Please," he said. He wanted to meet her gaze. He wanted to ask for her forgiveness. She would have never gotten hurt if he hadn't left her like that.

She studied him for a moment but then nodded. "Okay," she whispered.

Jonathan's heart was hammering in his chest as he carried her to his car and opened the door. He set her down gently into the front seat and moved to buckle her in, but she beat him to it.

Just as he pulled his hand away to shut her door, Tiffany grabbed him. "Hey," she said. Her voice was low and raspy—no doubt from the salt water she'd consumed. "I'm okay. Really."

Jonathan flexed his jaw as he stared down at her. His

body coursed with fear and joy—a strange combination. It was causing his stomach to tie into knots. He could have lost his best friend. She could have died. What would he have done then? He would have never been able to forgive himself.

Worried that his voice might break if he spoke, Jonathan just nodded and then shut the door behind him.

He fisted his hands as he rounded the hood to climb into the driver's seat. They drove in silence toward Honey Grove General, where he pulled into the parking lot and turned off the engine.

Tiffany was out of the car by the time he jogged around to help her out. He dipped down to scoop her up, but she gave him a death stare.

"I can walk in there on my own," she said, lowering her voice to sound threatening.

Jonathan contemplated ignoring her and scooping her up into his arms anyway. After all, she was about as heavy as a feather. But he decided to just nod and step out of her way. He'd keep a close eye on her, and if he saw any sign of struggle, he'd ignore her insistence and help her out.

Two hours later, Jonathan followed her out of the hospital. After some tests, they said she should be watched but that she could go home. Jonathan nodded, listening to everything the doctor said.

When they climbed into his car, Jonathan glanced over at her. "Anyone at your apartment tonight?" he asked.

Tiffany sighed. "I'm fine Jonathan. I'll be fine. I can spend the night in my apartment. Alone."

Jonathan started the engine and pulled out of the parking lot. "The doctor said—"

"I don't care what the doctor said. I'm fine. You can stop treating me like something that's broken."

Jonathan tightened his grip on the steering wheel as he

narrowed his eyes. Sure, Tiffany was strong. But with something like this, her strength was irritating. It was a wall she'd built up around her heart ever since her parents left her. To her, letting someone in was a sign of weakness.

She didn't want to appear to care about anything, because then she could never be hurt. It frustrated him that she was pulling this crap on him.

So, despite her insistence that he take her back to the Tavern to get her car, he drove her over to his house.

"Seriously, Jonathan?" she asked, twisting in her seat to stare at him.

"Come on. Just one night, then I'll leave you alone."

Tiffany's jaw dropped as she stared at his house and then back over to Jonathan. "And I get no say in this."

Jonathan shot her a smile as he grabbed the door handle and climbed out of his car. "Nope."

He watched her through the windshield as she sat there with her arms crossed over her chest. He could tell that she was frustrated, but he didn't care. It was his fault that she was in this mess, and it was his job to make sure she was okay.

He pulled on her door handle and waited. Finally, she climbed out—but not before she gave him an annoyed look—and he shut the door behind her.

They walked in silence up to the house and into the kitchen.

His mom was sitting at the table and reading a book when they walked in. Her eyes widened as she took in their appearance.

"What happened to you two?" she asked, standing up and coming over.

"We went swimming and Tiffany almost drowned," Jonathan said.

Sondra glanced between them and then ushered Tiffany

farther into the house. "Oh my goodness, come inside, sweetheart. Let me get you some tea."

Tiffany walked past Jonathan, ignoring him as she went. Then she glanced over at his mom. "Actually, I'd love to just take a shower. I've got sand everywhere."

Sondra wrapped her arm around Tiffany's shoulders and nodded. "Of course. Jonathan?"

Even though he was frustrated that his mom was taking over, Jonathan pushed aside his feelings and joined them. "Yeah?"

"Take her upstairs and help her get the things she needs."

Jonathan let out his breath and nodded. "Of course."

He went to rest his hand on her lower back, but Tiffany moved away before he could touch her. She grabbed onto the railing and made her way up the stairs before he could say anything.

"I know the way," she said over her shoulder without even looking back.

Jonathan watched her retreat. He could feel her frustration as she walked away. He knew she didn't want to stay here, but he hadn't realized it would make her this upset.

He glanced over to his mom. She had a concerned expression on her face.

"You okay?" she asked, walking over to wrap her arm around his shoulders.

The weight of the evening bore down on him. It had been so terrifying, staring at Tiffany's lifeless body. Worrying that she might be gone.

"Yeah," he said, his voice breaking.

Sondra pulled him into a hug and held him. "She's fine."

Jonathan forced away the tears that built up in his eyes and cleared his throat. "Yeah, I just hope she doesn't kill me in my sleep. She's not too excited about our little sleepover."

Sondra chuckled as she pulled back. "That doesn't

surprise me. Tiffany has never liked to be forced to do anything."

Jonathan pushed his hands through his hair and nodded. The feeling of sand and saltwater coated his whole body. He glanced toward the basement. "I'm going to take a shower downstairs."

Sondra patted him on the back. "All righty. I'll bring you two some cookies and tea when you're done."

Jonathan thanked his mom and slipped into the basement, where he was determined to wash off the beach and the stress of the evening.

CHAPTER FOUR

Tiffany stood in the shower as the hot water beat down on her. She leaned against the wall, and the water washed away the stress of the night. She didn't remember much of what happened after swimming away from the island, there was just a jabbing pain in her side and the rest was a blur.

She could handle pain. That had become second nature to her. But what was playing over and over in her mind was the terrified expression on Jonathan's face when she'd come to.

She'd felt his fear, and that was almost as terrifying as the thought that she'd almost drowned. And it wasn't helping that he was doting on her like a broken china doll.

She wanted things to go back to normal—no, she *needed* them to. Not only did Sean break her heart, but now her best friend was acting weird around her. She prided herself on being able to take care of herself, and having Jonathan insist on doing things for her was bringing out a side of her that she didn't like. But she couldn't help it. She was so used to being the one thing standing between her and a broken heart.

And when her father left, saying he was relieved to dump the burden that had been dragging him down, she couldn't help but project that onto every aspect of her life. She couldn't be a burden to the people she loved. She just couldn't. Jonathan loved her as a friend now, but what was she going to do when he decided that he didn't? Rejection from him wasn't something she could come back from. If he left her, too, she'd have no one.

Sighing, she grabbed the shampoo and lathered it up. Once she was clean, she grabbed a towel to wrap up her hair and then wrapped another around her body.

She stepped out onto the plush bathmat and wiped at the fog on the mirror in front of her. After staring at her blotchy skin and tired eyes, she sighed and opened the door. Just as she was about to walk out, Jonathan appeared.

He'd showered as well and was now wearing a t-shirt and sweatpants. His eyebrow raised as his gaze roamed over her. Her skin heated from the intensity of his gaze. Then, as quickly as it came, he dropped it and cleared his throat. "Here's some pajamas," he said, holding them out for her.

Tiffany took the stack of clothes. "Thanks," she said. For the first time, she felt very aware of the fact that she was wearing only a towel.

Since when did she care about that around Jonathan? He was her friend. That was it.

She was more than ready to get to bed and sleep off the weirdness of this whole evening. So she turned and made her way back into the bathroom, where she slipped into his old t-shirt and gym shorts.

After pulling her hair up into a messy bun at the top of her head, she forced herself not to look at the mirror. No need to see what she already knew—she was a hot mess.

She opened up the bathroom door and turned off the light. She made her way down the hall to the guest bedroom.

"Where are you going?" Jonathan asked.

Tiffany stopped and slowly turned. "The guest room."

Jonathan shook his head. "Not tonight. Doc said I have to keep an eye on you. You're bunking with me." He pointed his finger toward his room, as if that was all it was going to take to get her in there.

She folded her arms. "Are you trying to get me into your bed?" she asked.

Jonathan's cheeks flushed as he cleared his throat and shoved his hands into his pockets. "Um. No."

Startled by his reaction, Tiffany let out a laugh. "I was just joking." Realizing that she may have crossed a line, she walked over to him. "I know you see me as a sister," she said as she punched his arm.

Jonathan winced and nodded. "Of course."

Ignoring the fact that his words sounded slightly forced, she made her way into his room. It hadn't changed much since they were kids. Except for the treadmill in the corner.

"Yours?" she asked as she made her way over to the bed and sat down.

Jonathan smiled and shook his head. "Naw, that's Dad's."

She nodded as she scooted back against the headboard.

"Knock knock." Tiffany turned to see Mrs. Braxton make her way into the room. Her gaze roamed over Tiffany and a smile emerged on her lips. "You look better. That shower did you some good."

Tiffany nodded. "It was needed." She'd always liked Mrs. Braxton. She'd always acted like a second mother to Tiffany since her actual mother was some deadbeat who'd left her when things got hard.

Mrs. Braxton set a plate of cookies and two steaming mugs on the nightstand next to Tiffany then she straightened and glanced around.

"Well, then. I'll leave you two to your sleep." She turned

and stuck her finger against Jonathan's chest. "I'm right down the hall," she said in a tone that sounded more threatening than informative.

Jonathan held up his hands. "We're just going to be sleeping."

Mrs. Braxton narrowed her eyes. "Better be."

Confused by the feelings that crept up in her stomach at Mrs. Braxton's implication, Tiffany reached over and grabbed a cookie. Maybe it was better if she just focused on eating, instead of dissecting the whole vibe of the room.

Once Mrs. Braxton was gone, the air around them lightened. Jonathan made his way over to his old closet and grabbed out a few extra blankets and began shaking them out onto the floor.

"What are you doing?" Tiffany asked as she peeked over at him.

"I've got to sleep somewhere."

Noting the size of the twin mattress underneath her, Tiffany nodded. "Yeah. You're too big to fit on here with me."

"Yep." Then he hesitated. "Should I be worried about my weight or something? This is the second time you've talked about my size." He glanced in the mirror above the dresser on the other side of the room and then turned to the side, sucking in his stomach.

Tiffany rolled her eyes and chucked a pillow in his direction. "You couldn't pinch an inch if you wanted to."

The pillow slammed into his back, and Jonathan turned and shot her a fake hurt look. "Oh, it's on," he said, grabbing the pillow and diving at her.

Squealing, Tiffany reached for another pillow as protection. She held it up, but it was futile. Jonathan was much stronger. She crawled to the corner of the bed and held up her pillow. "I surrender!" she exclaimed. Her sides hurt from laughter.

This was what she needed. Getting back to their easy relationship made her feel better. Like she wasn't a weight wrapped around Jonathan's neck, dragging him down.

Jonathan threw his pillow down to the ground and collapsed on the bed. He rolled onto his side and propped his head on his hand. His laughter died down, and a serious expression passed over his face.

Nerves built up inside of Tiffany, so she pulled her knees to her chest and rested her chin on them. Gathering her courage, she met his gaze.

The pain and guilt there almost took her breath away. Jonathan had been worried about her. Reaching out, she grabbed onto his hand and held it. Warmth raced up her skin and exploded in her body.

"I'm okay," she said, surprised at the depth in her voice.

Jonathan dropped his gaze and studied their hands. Then he glanced back up at her. "I don't know what I would do if I lost you. You're my best friend."

Tiffany nodded, tears filling her eyes. "I know. I know. I'm sorry."

Jonathan fell silent and then flipped to his back. He pulled his hand away to rest it on his chest. She could see his slow and steady breathing. In a weird way, it was really calming.

"That was weird, huh?" he asked.

Confused, she turned her gaze up to the ceiling. "What?"

Jonathan closed his lips and silence filled the air. Finally, he spoke after what felt like an eternity. "What my mom was implying."

Tiffany almost choked on her tongue. "You mean about the two of us?" It was almost too weird to even talk about hypothetically.

Jonathan nodded.

Tiffany had no idea what she was supposed to say to that. That was one place she'd never gone to. Jonathan was just that. *Jonathan.* She'd never allowed herself to think of him in that way.

"I—um..." Nothing wanted to leave her lips that made any sense, so she decided the best thing to do was to shut them and never speak again.

Jonathan laughed as he sat up. "I'm just joking," he said as he turned and shoved her shoulder. "Geez, you should see your face. You're white as a ghost."

A relieved laugh escaped her lips. She reached out and shoved his shoulder. "Don't ever do that again, weirdo," she said, grabbing a pillow and flopping down onto it. She then pressed her feet against him, hoping he'd get the hint.

Jonathan's chuckle filled the air as he slipped from the bed and onto the floor. After a few minutes, the sound of him adjusting the blankets subsided and silence filled the air.

Even though it was weird to talk about them being anything but best friends, there was still this strange feeling rising up in her stomach. Their duo had almost stopped today. And Jonathan had been the one to save her.

"Jonathan?" she asked as she stared up at the dark ceiling above her.

"Yeah?"

"I don't think I ever thanked you for saving my life. So...thanks."

Silence. Had she said the wrong thing? She turned onto her side to peek over the edge of the mattress.

Jonathan sighed. "You don't ever have to thank me for something like that. You're my best friend, and I'm here to protect you. Now, go to sleep."

Tiffany felt a smile spread across her lips as she bunched her blanket up in her arms and hugged it to her chest. What Jonathan had said was true. Despite the people that came in and out of their lives, they were always friends, and nothing was ever going to change that.

The sun beat in through the window the next morning, pulling Tiffany from her sleep. She groaned and twisted, hoping to bury her face in her blankets.

Suddenly, a pillow whacked her in the face, and she bolted up. "Hey," she said, grabbing the pillow and throwing it back at Jonathan.

He sat up, rubbing his eyes, sleep still clinging to his gaze. "What are you doing, crazy lady?" he asked as he grabbed the pillow and threw it back.

Just as she grabbed it to retaliate, Jonathan stood and pulled it from her.

"Let me take that for you," he said, holding it high in the air.

Tiffany glared at him. "You couldn't have let me sleep for a few minutes longer?"

Jonathan fluffed the pillow and then set it at the head of his makeshift bed. "I smell bacon and pancakes. Mom's cooking breakfast, and it's best fresh."

Tiffany cheered as she pulled off the blankets and slipped her feet onto the floor. "Race you there?" she squealed as she rushed past him and over to the door.

"Cheater!" Jonathan exclaimed, but that didn't stop Tiffany. Instead, she raced down the stairs and into the kitchen where she saw a very wide-eyed Sondra.

Her gaze swept over Tiffany. "Did you sleep well, sweetheart?"

Tiffany nodded, suddenly realizing that she'd just slept over at Jonathan's house and had no idea what she looked like. Feeling self-conscious, she reached up and began to run her fingers through her hair, wincing as she caught a few snarls along the way.

The sound of Jonathan's feet clomping down the stairs

caused her to move away and over to the corner.

"Ma, will you tell Tiffany that cheaters are not allowed in the Braxton house?" Jonathan asked, winking at Tiffany as he folded his arms.

Sondra tapped her chin. "Did she call out the start of the race?"

Jonathan shook his head.

"I did too," Tiffany said, stepping closer to him.

Sondra shrugged as she wiped her hands on her apron and returned to the griddle where bacon was crackling. "Seems legit to me."

Jonathan dropped his jaw and then turned to Tiffany. "It's on," he mouthed.

The sound of a bowl clattering in the sink drew Jonathan's attention. Tiffany followed his gaze to see Mrs. Braxton standing over the sink, her shoulders slumped as she stared at it.

"You okay, Ma?" Jonathan asked as he walked over and wrapped his arm around her shoulders.

Realizing that she'd been so selfish, Tiffany walked over to her.

Mrs. Braxton sighed as she glanced at both of them. "Grandpa's having health problems. I'm going to need to head to Jordan to help."

Jonathan nodded. "Anything we can do?"

Mrs. Braxton shook her head. "No. Josh is running my jam booth at the fair."

Tiffany glanced up at Jonathan. He dropped his gaze. "We can help out, too. We'll go over as soon as we can."

Mrs. Braxton turned and wrapped her arms around Jonathan. "It's so good to have you home," she said, her voice muffled by his shoulder.

Jonathan patted her back. "It's good to be back."

After Mrs. Braxton slipped on her shoes, she shouldered her purse and gave him a wave. "I'll see you two tonight?"

Jonathan glanced over at Tiffany. "Probably."

A content look passed over her face as she smiled. "Perfect."

Once she was gone, Tiffany slipped onto a chair at the table and dished up a few pancakes. She poured syrup on them and watched from the corner of her eye as Jonathan walked over to the coffee pot and began to fill up a mug.

"Oh, get me one too," she said, pointing her fork at him.

Jonathan quirked an eyebrow but nodded. Once a second mug was filled, he carried it over to her and set it down.

They sat in silence. Jonathan filled a plate and dug in while Tiffany sipped her coffee.

It felt nice, sitting next to Jonathan. For some reason, she never felt like she had to fill the silence. Being with Jonathan felt as natural as breathing.

"What?" Jonathan asked with his mouth full of pancake.

Tiffany shrugged as a smile spread across her lips. "Nothing. I'm just glad you're back."

Jonathan's expression softened as he studied her. Then he gave her a wink and stabbed his pancakes with his fork. "I'm happy too."

She stuck out her hand. "Friends forever?"

Jonathan studied her hand and then met it, shaking it exaggeratedly. "Friends forever. Now, can we eat?"

Tiffany nodded. "Of course."

CHAPTER FIVE

The warm South Carolina air surrounded Jonathan as he stood next to the Ferris wheel. The sun had gone down, which was nice. All of his sweat had dried, leaving him with a caked-in-salt feeling.

They'd spent the afternoon at the fair. His nephew Jordan had kept them busy with games and rides, but now Josh had insisted that Jordan stay with him at the booth. Last Jonathan checked, Jordan was passed out on a makeshift bed under a table.

Pushing his hand through his hair, he glanced over at Tiffany, who was studying her phone.

She didn't look happy.

"What's up?" he asked, tapping her phone with his finger.

Tiffany glanced up at him. "Nothing," she said, shoving her phone into her pocket.

Jonathan quirked an eyebrow. "Nothing?"

She reached up and tightened her ponytail and forced a smile. Then, as if she realized that she could never lie to him, she let out her breath. "It's my cousin's wedding. I was supposed to go next weekend, and now…" She rubbed her temples. "I can't go without Sean."

Confused, Jonathan studied her. "What? Why?"

Tiffany glanced over at him. "I can't go without a date," she whispered.

Jonathan leaned in. "A date?" he asked, just to make sure he'd heard her right.

Tiffany nodded. "My family is cutthroat, and I'm the pariah. All my cousins are married with five kids." She waved to herself. "Loser."

Jonathan chuckled. It was nice hearing that he wasn't the only one who's family harassed them because of their relationship status. He leaned in to study her forehead.

Tiffany pulled back, her eyes wide. "What are you doing?"

"I'm searching for the 'L' on your face."

Tiffany rolled her eyes and shoved his shoulder. "You know, for a best friend, you suck."

Jonathan grabbed her arms and pulled her closer. A wash of warmth cascaded over him as her soft skin registered against his palms. As if he'd been shocked with electricity, Jonathan dropped his hands and stepped back.

Tiffany furrowed her brow. Worried that he looked like an idiot, Jonathan stepped over to the nearby churro vendor and ordered two.

He handed one over to Tiffany, and they filled the silence with eating.

Then an idea formed in his mind. He swallowed and cleared his throat, drawing Tiffany's attention over.

"How about I go with you?" he asked, shrugging his shoulders as if he didn't care what she said.

Tiffany snorted. "As what, my friend? Yeah, I'll look like an even bigger dork."

"Ouch."

Tiffany shook her head. "Not because of you. Are you

serious? My family will probably string me up if they found out that my best friend is in the NFL." She chuckled. "I can already hear my aunts now: *he's such a man, how can you stay away?*"

Jonathan's eyes widened. "Good to know that's how you see me," he said, lifting his arms and flexing.

Tiffany swatted at his arms. "Put those away. You're going to hurt someone."

Jonathan laughed but then he grew serious. If he couldn't help his friend, what good was he? Besides, it sounded nice to get away. "Come on, I'll be your date. It can be just one single friend helping out another single friend. Besides, you can flaunt me in front of all of your friends."

Tiffany's expression grew contemplative as she studied him. Then she sighed. "I'll think about it."

Jonathan nodded and then waved over to the Ferris wheel. "Wanna go for a ride?" He was ready for a distraction.

Tiffany glanced at it and then over to him. "Definitely."

The ride attendant took his tickets and ripped them. Then he followed Tiffany to an empty bucket and climbed in. He tried to ignore the feeling of her leg pressed against his or of his arm as it brushed her.

All of this was very strange, and if Jonathan were being honest, he didn't like it.

Clearing his throat, he glanced over at her as he grabbed the safety bar that was pressed to their laps. Tiffany met his gaze with an amused expression on her face.

"What?" she asked.

Jonathan shrugged. "Nothing."

Tiffany settled back in her seat. "So, tell me about Pittsburgh. Anyone you're pining after there?"

Jonathan shrugged. "Nah. Women who know I'm a professional player treat me different."

Tiffany dropped her jaw in an exaggerated movement. "*I* don't."

"I didn't mean you," he said, reaching over and shoving her shoulder.

Tiffany gave him a strange look. "Why not me? I'm a woman. I see you." She leaned back as if to take him all in. Then she wiggled her eyebrows.

Not sure how he felt under Tiffany's scrutiny, Jonathan just shrugged. "Yeah, but we'll never see each other as anything other than friends."

When Tiffany didn't answer, Jonathan glanced over to see her staring at a couple a few buckets down. Focusing his attention on them, Jonathan squinted.

It looked like...Sean. And he had his face securely attached to another woman. Anger coursed through his veins as he glanced over at Tiffany, who'd dropped her gaze to her hands. He could tell she was fighting back tears.

"He's an idiot," Jonathan said, reaching around her and pulling her closer to him.

Tiffany rested her head on his shoulder as she nodded. "He's a jerk."

"He didn't know what he had." Jonathan reached out and cradled her free hand in his. His senses must have been heightened, because he'd never noticed how soft her skin was until today.

Strange.

Tiffany moved her fingers so she could lace them together with his. She sighed and Jonathan reveled in the sound.

He'd never noticed how feminine Tiffany was. And for some reason, he had this deep desire to protect her and confront Sean—or anything that threatened Tiffany's happiness.

"Jonathan," she whispered.

"Yeah?"

She tipped her head back to study him. Then her nose wrinkled. "You smell like a gym locker room." And then she smiled up at him. "But I bet I do too. Blast this summer heat."

Jonathan chuckled as he pulled his arm away from her. Embarrassment coursed through him, and he shrugged. "Sorry."

She giggled. "It's okay."

They spent the rest of the time talking about their plans for the summer. Nothing too deep, just surface level. When they got off the ride, they took their time to glare at Sean, whose eyebrows rose when he finally looked over and noticed them.

Tiffany reached out and slipped her hand into Jonathan's as they passed. Even though he was just fine helping Tiffany save face, his body decided to react to her touch.

His heart began to pound as he held her dainty hand in his own.

Confused with what that meant, Jonathan decided to push it from his mind.

This was Tiffany he was thinking about.

The next morning, Jonathan stretched out in his bed. He rested his hand on his chest as he stared up at the ceiling. His thoughts were swirling as he recounted the strange reaction he'd had last night. After the ride, they spent some time with Beth, listening to the live band at the fair. He'd needed that though. It'd been too confusing to try to process what was going on in his body.

Jonathan flexed his hand. The memory of Tiffany's hand in his seemed burned in his mind. What did that mean?

Clearing his throat, he threw off the covers and made his way to the bathroom.

Nothing. It meant nothing. He was just confused.

After taking a hot shower, Jonathan wrapped a towel around his waist and flung open the bathroom door to find Tiffany on the other side, her eyes wide.

"I, um…" She cleared her throat as her gaze flicked down to his chest and then back up to his eyes.

A satisfied feeling rose up inside of him as he crossed his arms and leaned against the door frame. "Always looking for a way to see me without a shirt on," he said giving her a wink and then reveling in the blush that rushed to her cheeks.

Tiffany scowled. "Well, it's hard not to stare," she said, reaching out and pressing her finger to his muscles.

Jonathan chuckled. "Always got to touch them."

Tiffany curled her finger back into her palm and dropped her hand. She glared at him. "Well, I was going to ask you to come to the wedding with me, but now, I'm not so sure."

A rush of excitement ran through him as Jonathan pushed off the door frame. "What? Why?"

She quirked an eyebrow. "You're being flirty right now, when we're *not* faking a relationship. How are you going to act when we are? I can't imagine this magnified." She motioned between them.

Jonathan crossed his heart. "I promise, no excessive flirting." He clasped his hands together in a pleading motion. "Take me with you. It'll be fun. Besides, I'm sure you have some cute, single cousins who could help me get through our breakup." He winked at her, and Tiffany rolled her eyes. "You'd be doing me a solid, Tiff. From the way my mom is going on and on, if I don't get someone on my arm ASAP, I'm pretty sure I'll be written out of the will."

Tiffany's smile faltered for a moment, but then she smiled, making Jonathan wonder if he'd even seen anything.

She sighed and rolled her eyes. "Fine. You can come with me."

Jonathan pumped his fists in the air. "Awesome."

Tiffany studied him with a smile on her lips. "You're such a dork."

Jonathan stepped forward, reveling in the feeling of her body next to his, and his body sparked with the thought of touching her. Worried about what that meant, Jonathan stepped past her, breaking the strange current of electricity that seemed to be running between them.

"I should get dressed," he said.

"Yeah. I was going to say the same. Your mom said to tell you that breakfast's ready," Tiffany said as she turned and made her way down the stairs.

Jonathan dressed in a t-shirt and gym shorts. When he entered the kitchen, he kissed his mom on the cheek and then smiled at his dad. It was good to be home. So familiar and exactly what he needed.

He sat down next to Tiffany as he ruffled Jordan's hair. "What are you doing here, squirt?" he asked.

Jordan ducked out of the way. "Eating," he said, syrup dripping from his chin.

Jonathan chuckled as he grabbed some pancakes from the stack in front of him. "You can't keep cooking like this, Ma. I'm going to be 300 pounds when I go back."

Sondra just chuckled. "It's good for you. Energy."

Jonathan drizzled his pancakes with syrup as he shook his head. Leave it to his mom to make cakes doused in sugar healthy.

The conversation around the table remained light as everyone ate their breakfast. Right when Jordan demanded another stack of pancakes, Josh burst into the kitchen. He looked confused and frustrated.

"Hey, sweetie," Sondra said. "Hungry?"

"For your pancakes? You bet."

Sondra's smile widened as she grabbed a clean plate and began stacking pancakes onto it. "Great. I've got more batter."

Jonathan eyed his brother. He was confused by Josh's agitation. But, before he could ask, Sondra placed a plate down next to him and Josh grabbed the syrup.

"Your pancakes can heal the soul, Ma," Josh said as he shoved a bite into his mouth.

"Heal the soul? Why does your soul need to be healed?" Sondra asked, as she turned and shot him a strange look.

Jonathan studied his brother. He'd definitely sensed something last night between Josh and Beth, could that be what was bugging him?

Josh just shrugged in his familiar noncommittal gesture. "No reason."

Jonathan wanted to tease his brother. It was such a common reaction to his brothers. Especially when they were acting weird. Glancing over at Tiffany, Jonathan saw her give Josh a strange look. Like there was something she wanted to say but couldn't.

By the time he returned his gaze to Josh, he saw his brother staring at him. "How's the team?" Josh asked as he shoved another forkful of food into his mouth.

Relieved to talk about anything other than what was happening in the room, Jonathan filled the silence with facts and stats about the Steelers. Never mind the fact that there was a chance he could be traded. Right now, he wanted to think and talk about something he understood. And he understood football.

"Beth's mom has cancer," Tiffany blurted out, drawing Jonathan's attention over to her.

Why would she say that?

Josh stopped mid-bite to stare at Tiffany. "What?" he

asked at the same time as Sondra, who'd made her way over as well.

"Joanne has cancer. That's why Beth's been so standoffish," she said as she took a sip of milk.

Josh looked confused. "I thought she was seeing someone else."

Still confused, Jonathan glanced between Tiffany and his brother. What was going on here? How could this have been happening around him without him noticing?

Tiffany snorted. "Sorry, no. There's no one else."

Sondra was muttering under her breath. "No, no, that can't be right. I would know if Joanne was sick."

Jonathan wanted to add to the conversation but didn't know what to say. So, he just kept silent was he watched their interaction.

"Joanne wanted her to keep it a secret. It's been killing Beth."

"Is that where she's going this morning?" Josh asked.

Tiffany furrowed her brow. "If she needed a ride somewhere, that's probably where she was going. Her mom is in Jordan right now. At St. Jude's."

"St. Jude's? I was just there last night. I didn't see Joanne," Sondra said. "Poor Joanne. Why didn't she tell anyone?"

"I guess she didn't want everyone to feel sorry for her. She made Beth promise not to tell anyone."

Jonathan felt as if he were intruding on a conversation that he wasn't a part of. So instead of staring at everyone who was talking, he decided to focus on his food.

"Can I go watch cartoons?" Jordan asked. Jonathan watched as Josh excused him, and he couldn't help but want to go with him.

Jonathan wanted to help Josh, but he didn't know how. A few minutes later, Josh stood and practically rushed from the house. Sondra followed after him, shutting the outside door behind her.

The kitchen fell silent as Jonathan glanced over to Tiffany. She was staring at the table top, her forehead wrinkled.

Wanting to comfort her, Jonathan reached out and rested his hand on her shoulder. "How long have you known?" he asked.

Tiffany heaved a sigh, her breath causing his hand to move up and down. "Just a little bit. She's been keeping it a secret from me as well. If I hadn't walked in when I did, I wouldn't have known."

Jonathan reached over to grab his milk. "Yeah. It's hard when people keep secrets from you."

Tiffany pushed her pancakes around on her plate. "Agreed." Then she turned and held out her pinky. "Promise you won't ever keep things a secret from me?"

Jonathan stared at her finger. "Isn't that a little juvenile?"

Tiffany shook her head. "It never failed us in the past, and I'm not going to let it fail us now." Then she narrowed her eyes. "Promise?"

A worried feeling crept up into Jonathan's stomach, but he pushed it down. It wasn't like he'd ever kept a secret from her before; why was he worried he'd start now?

So he nodded and wrapped his pinky around hers. "I promise."

Tiffany tightened her finger as she narrowed her eyes. Then a smile played on her lips and she turned back to her phone.

"Oh, by the way, I told my aunt that you're coming. So… be prepared."

Relieved to be talking about something other than secrets and his brother's romantic life, Jonathan grabbed his fork and nodded. "Good. That's good, right?"

Tiffany shot him a sympathetic look. "Oh, you're so innocent," she said, smiling at him in a slightly sadistic way.

Jonathan studied her as he finished off the pancakes on his plate. "Should I be worried?"

Tiffany fell silent. Then she glanced up at him. "Just be prepared."

"It's on Saturday?" he asked as he stood and brought his plate to the sink.

Tiffany nodded. "Yep. But we need to be there Friday afternoon. Lots of wedding festivities we need to participate in."

Jonathan turned and leaned against the counter. "I'm sure I can handle whatever your family throws at me."

Tiffany stepped forward and patted him on the cheek. "I hope so."

She giggled as she walked toward the living room, where the sound of Jordan's cartoons could be heard. Jonathan watched her walk away. He brushed off her doom-and-gloom attitude and sighed.

He could survive a weekend with her family. He was sure of it. After all, how hard could it be?

CHAPTER SIX

Tiffany clutched her purse to her side as she bounced a few times on the balls of her feet. Where was Jonathan? She paced in front of her apartment, her gaze whipping over when the sound of a passing car distracted her.

How could he be late? She'd spent the entire week reminding him that she needed to be picked up at 10 a.m. sharp on Friday. Jonathan would pull his typical, *you mean Saturday*, routine, but she'd just punched his arm in response.

Now that he was fifteen minutes late, she was starting to worry that, with all his teasing, he'd confused himself.

Just as she reached into her purse to call him, his Jaguar sped into her apartment complex, and he threw it into park. Before she could blink, he was out of the car and over to her, with a guilty look written all over his face.

"I'm so sorry. Mom wanted us to have food for the road, and she took forever to get it ready."

Tiffany rolled her eyes. Typical Jonathan, blaming it on anyone but himself. "Really?" she asked as he grabbed her suitcase and threw it into the trunk.

Jonathan slammed the trunk shut and then turned to face her. "Really." He held up his hand. "I swear. I was ready to go, but she insisted. And I can't disappoint her."

Tiffany eyed him and then smiled. "Well, I hope it was worth it," she said as she pulled open the passenger door and the smell of freshly baked cookies wafted out. Her mouth instantly salivated as she nodded. "Oh, it was worth it."

Jonathan chuckled as he buckled his seatbelt. "I figured you'd feel that way."

Tiffany was already digging around in the back for the cooler she was sure held the cookies. Jonathan brushed past her as he leaned into the back as well. A warm feeling surrounded her as his chest touched her arm.

Startled, she pulled away. Glancing at the temperature dial in the car, she realized that it wasn't the heat in the car that had her temperature rising.

Shaking her head, she decided it was better to sit there than to try to find the cookies herself. Plus, Jonathan seemed to know exactly where they were. She folded her arms across her chest, and a few seconds later, Jonathan pulled a bag of cookies up to the front.

"Here you go," he said as he dropped them into her lap. Then he focused on starting the car and pulling out of her apartment complex.

The wedding was three hours away.

It didn't take long until Jonathan was on the highway, leaning back in his seat and resting his wrist on the steering wheel. Tiffany couldn't help but peek over at him. He looked so relaxed as he kept his focus on the road. He had sunglasses perched on his nose.

It wasn't until now that Tiffany realized he had a perfectly shaped nose…and lips.

Blinking back her thoughts, Tiffany turned her attention

to the road and decided that shoving her face full of cookies was the best use of her time.

"How long have you loved me?" Jonathan's voice startled her.

She inhaled her cookies, the crumbs flying to the back of her throat and throwing her into a coughing fit. "I don't love you," she wheezed as her eyes watered.

Once she'd cleared her throat of all cookie debris and had wiped her eyes, she felt Jonathan's gaze on her. His eyebrows were raised and his lips parted.

He occasionally flicked his gaze over to the road and then back to her. "Are you going to live?" he asked.

Frustrated, Tiffany nodded. Was he just messing with her? Had he heard her thought about his lips? "Yes," she said, her voice raspy.

He nodded. "Good. I wasn't sure how I was going to explain a dead Tiffany to your family." He snorted as he raised his hand. "Here lies Tiffany, she died eating a cookie."

Tiffany scoffed. Of course, Jonathan would make a joke at her expense when she almost died. "Good to know that's what was going through your mind when I sat here choking." She reached out and grabbed his water bottle and took a swig.

"Geez, you ask me to fake date you, accuse me of killing you, and steal my water." He glanced over his sunglasses at her. "Best relationship I've ever been in."

"Har har. You'd be lucky to be in a relationship with me." It felt strange to hear those words roll off her tongue. And she wasn't sure how she felt about that.

When Jonathan didn't say anything, Tiffany peeked over at him. Had she taken it too far? He didn't look upset or uncomfortable, so Tiffany just shrugged off the strange feeling creeping up inside of her.

She was taking things too literally and she needed to stop right now.

Taking her resolve literally, Tiffany leaned back in her chair and brought her feet up to rest on the dash. She got out her phone and began playing around on it.

"I was thinking we should come up with a backstory in case people ask us," Jonathan said, glancing over at her.

"Was that what your question was about?"

Jonathan chuckled. "Yep."

Tiffany sighed. "Well, good news is we've known each other basically our entire lives, so that is in our favor."

Jonathan nodded as he flipped on his blinker to pass a slow semi. "Right. You've always had a crush on me, and one day, you decided to throw caution to the wind and kiss me." He glanced over at her, and even though his sunglasses were dark, she could see him wink at her.

Great.

"Um, that's not how I remember it. You've always been in love with *me*. Pining after me. Writing love notes that you never sent. And then one day, you decided to tell me by singing to me outside my apartment until I came down." Tiffany tapped her chin. "And wasn't there someone throwing rotten tomatoes at you to get you to stop?"

Jonathan dropped his jaw. "Wow. You think my singing's that bad?"

Tiffany shrugged as she shifted so that her legs were crisscrossed in front of her. "I'm just going off the reaction of the audience, babe." She turned to him and batted her eyelashes.

Jonathan's expression stilled as he glanced over at her. Then his lips tipped up into a smile.

Not sure where she was going to take their conversation, Tiffany reached over and turned on the radio. She could count on one hand the times she'd felt awkward around

Jonathan, so the fact that it was becoming a regular occurrence was throwing her off.

Thankfully, she was saved by the oldies station and spent the rest of the trip belting out eighties classics.

Jonathan joined her for a couple, but for the most part, he spent the drive glancing over at her and rolling his eyes.

They pulled into the wrap-around driveway at Hotel Debonair, and Jonathan turned off the car. Standing outside the entrance was a man in a suit with his hair slicked back. When he saw them, he rushed over to the driver's side door and helped Jonathan open it up.

"Good afternoon, sir," he said as Jonathan stepped out. Tiffany followed suit, and soon they were both standing by the car.

"My name is Horace, and I'd be happy to park your car," he said, reaching his hand out for Jonathan's key.

"Horace, perfect," Jonathan said, handing the key over. "Let me grab out our suitcases first."

Horace held up his hand. "No need. We will be more than happy to bring your luggage up to your room. Last name?"

Jonathan clapped Horace on the back. It was quite comical how tall Jonathan was compared to Horace. And when he touched Horace, the poor man's frame literally shook.

"Braxton," Jonathan said and then turned and made his way over to Tiffany. "Wow. Nice place," he said, extending his elbow for Tiffany to take.

"Yeah. That's my family. Lavish as always." Tiffany slipped her arm through his.

Jonathan nodded and began to walk toward the front doors, which slid open with ease. "Now, remember," Jonathan said, his voice barely a whisper, "you're madly in love me." He glanced down at her, giving her a wink.

Tiffany snorted. "I'm a pretty good actress," she replied,

trying to ignore the butterflies that were floating around in her stomach. She was just nervous about seeing her family. That was all.

Plus, it'd only been a week since she broke up with Sean and had seen him kissing another girl. Her emotions were all out of whack.

"Tippy!" The familiar shrill voice of her cousin Stacy caused Tiffany to wince. Before she could brace herself, Stacy rammed into her and nearly crushed her rib cage.

Tiffany staggered a bit, but thankfully Jonathan was there. He pressed his hand into her lower back to keep her upright.

Once she had her bearings and breath back, Tiffany pulled away from Stacy. "Hey, Stace," she said, smiling at her cousin, whose dark brown eyes were bright with enthusiasm.

She grabbed onto Tiffany's arm and squeezed. "I'm getting married tomorrow," she squealed, jumping up and down, her dark brown hair swishing with the movement.

"Yep, you are," Tiffany said as she jumped along with Stacy.

Then, as if Stacy suddenly realized that Tiffany wasn't alone, her gaze fell on Jonathan and she stopped moving. Leaning forward, she met Tiffany's gaze. "Is this Sean?"

Not wanting to discuss that loser, Tiffany shook her head. "Nope. This is Jonathan."

Stacy gave Tiffany an approving look and then stepped past her and extended her hand. "Welcome, Jonathan," she breathed. Tiffany wasn't sure, but she thought Stacy had batted her eyelashes.

Typical.

Jonathan looked amused as he shook her hand. "Thanks for letting me come."

Stacy's gaze was fixated on Jonathan's hand and then moved up to Jonathan's arm, her smile widening as she went. "It's just great," she said.

Realizing that her cousin wasn't going to let him go, Tiffany stepped up to them and rested her hand on Jonathan's arm. "Stacy, where's Rob?"

"Who?"

"Rob? Your fiancé?"

Stacy stared at Tiffany as if the words weren't registering. Then she leaned forward with a giggle. "Oh, Rob. Yes. Rob. My fiancé. He's with his dad on the golf course right now."

Tiffany pulled Jonathan's hand free from Stacy's grasp and then threaded her fingers through his. Anything to keep Stacy's focus on something other than Jonathan.

From the corner of her eye, she could see Jonathan glance down at their intertwined hands. His attention caused her heart to pound. It must be the nerves she was feeling about seeing her whole family. And the fact that Stacy was hitting on her friend.

Claiming Jonathan as hers seemed to help snap Stacy out of her trance because she glanced over at Tiffany and smiled. "How was the drive?"

"Great. Smooth."

Stacy's gaze flicked over to Jonathan and then back to Tiffany. "You know what, I'm glad you brought Jonathan. Ted, Rob's cousin, called and said he can't make it." She glanced back over at Jonathan. "Would you mind filling in?"

Jonathan shifted, pressing his hand to chest. "Me?"

Stacy smiled and flicked her hair. "Of course. You'd fit right in."

Jonathan glanced down at Tiffany, and she shrugged. "If you want to, it's okay with me."

Jonathan nodded. "Sure. I'd need a tux though."

"Well it's a good thing they're waiting for Rob's brother to get in before they head to the shop. I'm sure they can find something for you."

Jonathan smiled. "Perfect. I'm happy to help."

Stacy let out a very loud giggle just as Horace walked up. "Mr. and Mrs. Braxton, here is your room key. Your luggage has been put in the room."

Jonathan took the two keycards from Horace but didn't correct the man. Not sure how she felt about being addressed as Mrs. Braxton, Tiffany stepped forward, parting her lips.

But Jonathan just squeezed her hand and pulled her back. Tiffany glanced up at him and he shook his head.

"Well, we should go freshen up and then we'll be back down," Jonathan said as he tugged on Tiffany's hand and stepped toward the elevator.

"All right!" Stacy called after them. "I'll let Rob know you're on board," she said as the elevator doors closed on her enthusiastic smile.

Once they were alone, Jonathan dropped Tiffany's hand. She stared down at her fingers, wondering why she could still feel the warmth of his hand and the pressure of his skin against hers.

Then, feeling like an idiot, she pushed all those thoughts away. What was the matter with her?

"You didn't have to do that," she said, glancing up at him.

Jonathan's lips were tipped up into a smile. "What?"

"Agree to help out at the wedding. You're already doing so much by coming as my date. I hate that you're being dragged into being a groomsman."

Jonathan leaned against the wall of the elevator and shrugged. "It's fine. No big deal, really. I'm happy to help out."

Tiffany eyed him. Was he telling the truth? He seemed to be. He didn't look like he was in distress. In fact, his shoulders were relaxed as he studied the numbers that were climbing.

Maybe he really was okay with this.

Tiffany sighed. "Well, if there's anything I can do to return the favor, let me know."

Jonathan glanced over and gave her his million-dollar smile. "Oh, I will."

The elevator dinged and the doors opened. Jonathan stepped out before Tiffany could ask what that meant. She rushed after him, realizing that she probably shouldn't have left that offer so open ended.

"Like what?" she asked, stepping up next to him as he pulled out the keycard and swiped the door.

He glanced over at her, but before he responded, he turned the door handle and stepped inside. The soft lighting shone against the gold wallpaper. A dark maroon comforter sat on the large bed. The cream carpet felt plush as she walked across it. It was hands down one of the fanciest hotels she'd ever stayed in.

Regret brewed in her stomach as Tiffany followed after him. She should have been more specific about how she would pay him back. "Like what?" she repeated.

Jonathan dive-bombed the bed—the only bed—and stretched out while propping himself up on one elbow. He was smiling, and she could see his teasing attitude in his gaze. But she'd moved on from their earlier conversation. Instead, she was inspecting the room, hoping that a second bed would magically appear in front of her.

"This is wrong," she muttered under her breath as she walked over to the phone and picked up the receiver. She'd asked for two beds, not one, when she'd changed her reservation last week. There was no way she could sleep in a bed with Jonathan, and she doubted that he wanted to sleep on the floor for the entire weekend.

The phone rang twice before a woman picked up. "Front desk, how may I help you?"

Tiffany rubbed her temples as she sat down on the desk

chair. "There's been a mistake. I asked for two beds. There's only one."

The clicking of keys sounded on the other end, and then the woman sighed. "It says we would try to make that accommodation, but we were unable to."

Frustration pricked at Tiffany's neck. "But—"

"Ma'am, we have a lot of guests this weekend, and we are fully booked. I'm so sorry. We can send up a cot, but it will cost extra."

Tiffany sighed. "No. That's fine. Thank you." She didn't wait for the woman to say goodbye. Instead, she hung up and glanced over at Jonathan, who was laying on his back, staring up at the ceiling.

"Everything okay?" he asked, glancing over at her.

Tiffany nodded as she made her way over to her suitcase and unzipped it. She needed something to do. Something to distract her. She didn't know why the thought of sharing a room with Jonathan had her this discombobulated. After grabbing a sundress, she made her way to the bathroom to change.

Just as she moved to shut the bathroom door, she glanced over at Jonathan. His eyes were closed and his hands were resting on his chest. She could see them rising and falling with his breath. There was something calming about watching him. The fact that he looked so relaxed helped her feel relaxed.

She shook her head as she shut the door. Maybe she was going insane.

Yeah, that was it. She was losing her mind.

CHAPTER SEVEN

Jonathan lay on the bed with his eyes closed. His muscles felt as if they were melting into the mattress. He tried not to read into the fact that Tiffany seemed upset to be sharing a room with him.

What did it matter?

It wasn't like they'd never slept in the same room together. Heck, they'd shared the same bed numerous times. So why would it suddenly bother her now?

Clearing his throat, he flipped off the bed and made his way over to the small sink in the hotel's kitchenette. If he lay there any longer, he was pretty sure he'd go mad from his own thoughts. It was probably best to distract himself.

He grabbed his suitcase and flung it onto the bed. With Tiffany in the bathroom, he'd take this time to change. He wasn't sure what was going on this evening but figured from the look of Tiffany's dress that it was fancier than his gym shorts and t-shirt allowed for.

He had some khaki pants on and was just about to slip on a button-down shirt when Tiffany opened the bathroom door. Her gaze landed on his bare chest and her cheeks flushed.

Suddenly self-conscious of the fact that he was standing there half-naked, Jonathan shot her an apologetic look, slipped his arms into his shirt, and began buttoning as fast as he could.

"Sorry. I thought I had a few more minutes before you got out," he said as he smoothed down his shirt.

Tiffany shook her head as she made her way into the room. "It's fine. It's not like I've never seen it before."

Jonathan had to bite his tongue. He wanted to tease her, but from the tension in the room, he figured it was probably not the smartest idea. Something was happening between him and Tiffany, and he wasn't sure what it was.

Teasing her was probably not the way to get to the bottom of it.

Tiffany busied herself with her makeup, so Jonathan grabbed his dress shoes and socks. Once he was ready, he styled his hair and then moved back over to the bed, sitting on the end of it.

Out of habit, his gaze made its way back over to Tiffany. She was leaning over the counter, bringing her face closer to the mirror. Jonathan couldn't help but notice the curves of her body. The way her floral dress flowed around her caused his body to warm.

He blinked a few times as he dropped his gaze. What was the matter with him? This was Tiffany he was thinking about. His best friend. In the past, he'd beat up guys that talked about Tiffany like this. Why was he doing it in his mind?

Needing to focus on something else, he grabbed his phone and started scrolling through it.

"So, do you know the plan for today?" he asked.

From the corner of his eye, he saw Tiffany turn to study

him. "There's a luncheon we are going to. And then after that, I think I go out for the final fitting of my dress. And since you're in the wedding party now, you'll go get your tux."

At the mention of food, Jonathan's stomach rumbled. "Food sounds like an amazing idea."

Tiffany nodded. "Figures."

Jonathan set his phone back onto the bed and turned to her. "I'm nothing if not consistent."

Tiffany laughed. It was soft and melodious. Why hadn't he ever noticed that before?

"Your cousin seems very welcoming." Distraction. That's what he needed.

Tiffany ran some red lipstick over her lips and then blotted them together. "Yeah. She is. She's a character."

Jonathan couldn't help but watch her as she strolled over to her suitcase and grabbed her sandals. She slipped one on, but just as she moved to push her foot into the second shoe, she stumbled.

Without thinking, Jonathan rushed over to help steady her. He rested one hand on her lower back and one on her upper arm.

As if shocked, Tiffany jumped away and straightened, staring over at him. "Wh-what are you doing?"

Jonathan's eyebrows shot up. Since when did he need a reason to help her? "I, um, didn't want you to fall." Was that wrong?

Tiffany nodded, her cheeks flushing as she bent down and grabbed her shoe and then made her way over to the bed to sit down.

Confused, Jonathan paced the room while he waited for her to finish getting ready. What was going on between them? It was like something was changing and he wasn't sure if he liked the direction it was going.

After her shoes were on, she stood and then nodded toward him as she made her way over to the door. "Let's go. Don't want to be late."

Jonathan nodded as he followed after her. Once they got into the elevator, they stood next to each other as the doors closed. Just before they fully shut, a hand appeared, along with a very breathy, "Wait."

Jonathan reached out and pressed the door open button. Thankfully, the elevator responded, and the doors slid back open.

A dark-haired woman appeared. Her eyes were just as dark as her hair and her cheeks were flushed. Her gaze met Jonathan's and her smile deepened. "Thanks," she said as she stepped into the elevator.

"No problem," Jonathan said as he hit the button for the doors to close.

"Haven't seen you in a while, Tiffany," the woman said as she turned and folded her arms. She tipped her gaze up to the numbers that were counting down the floors.

"Beatrice," Tiffany said.

Jonathan glanced between them. "Do you two know each other?"

Beatrice smiled at Jonathan. "We're cousins."

Jonathan did not get that. From the tension in the elevator, he'd pegged them more as mortal enemies. "Wow."

Beatrice kept her gaze on Jonathan until the elevator stopped moving and the doors opened. "And you are?" she asked as they stepped out. She turned and held her hand out to him.

"Jonathan," he said, taking her hand and shaking it.

"It's nice to meet you, Jonathan." She held his fingers for a moment longer than necessary.

Jonathan smiled and then tipped his head toward Tiffany. "I'm with her," he said.

Beatrice dropped his hand. "Of course. Well, I'll see you around."

Jonathan nodded. "Sounds good."

He watched at Beatrice made her way down the hall. Then he turned to see Tiffany glaring at him with her arms folded. He shrugged, trying not to melt under her scrutiny. "What?"

She shook her head. "Don't give me that. You were basically ogling my cousin." She started making her way down the hall once Beatrice disappeared.

"I was not ogling."

Tiffany snorted. "Yes, you were. I almost had to lift your jaw up off the ground." She glared at him as he kept pace with her.

"Wow. I'm sorry. I didn't know we were dating for real." He held up his hands.

Tiffany stopped. Her gaze was trained on the carpet. Realizing that he probably shouldn't have said that, he stepped forward and reached out to brush his fingers on her arm.

"I'm sorry—"

Tiffany glanced up at him with a forced smile. "No. You're right. We aren't dating. But if my family finds out that I brought a fake boyfriend to this wedding, I'll never live it down." She took a deep breath. "And there's stuff with Beatrice that I don't want to get into." She gave him a hopeful look. "Can you just keep your flirting tendencies in check and stay away from her?"

Jonathan studied her. Then he nodded. It was ridiculous that she even had to ask. She was his best friend, and he was here to help her out. "Of course. I'll be the best fake boyfriend a best friend could ever be." He stepped forward and wrapped his arm around her waist, pulling her close.

Zaps of electricity rushed across his skin at every point of contact. She was warm and soft and felt perfect, sandwiched against him. He couldn't help that his heart began pounding in his chest. Glancing down, he met her gaze. Her eyes were wide and her lips parted. He may have just found a way to stun Tiffany to silence.

"Your family will never see it coming," he said, making a conscious effort to lower his voice. He reached up and pushed her hair from her shoulder, exposing the hollows of her neck.

When she didn't respond, he glanced back over at her. Her cheeks were flushed and her heart was pounding.

"Tiffany?" he asked, hoping he hadn't gone too far.

She blinked a few times and then pushed away from him. She tucked her hair behind her ear and nodded. "Right. That sounds perfect." She slowly brought her gaze up to meet his and then held it for a moment before she turned. "Come on, we don't want to be late."

Jonathan followed after her as she led him down a few halls to the banquet room. Huge picture windows made up the far wall, and the afternoon sun spilled through, lighting up the entire room. Circle tables dotted the wood floor. Some were full of people, others only had one or two people sitting at them.

Along one wall, long tables sat covered in white tablecloths and platters of food. A line of people moved along them at a slow pace as they each dished themselves up.

"Hey, Jonathan!" Stacy's familiar voice grew louder as she neared. She was pulling a sunburned, red-haired man behind her. He was attempting to eat a croissant, but when she yanked on his arm, she pulled it away from his mouth.

"Rob, this is Jonathan, Tiffany's boyfriend. He agreed to be in the wedding party." Stacy gave him a huge smile as she peeked up at him.

Rob was about a foot shorter than Jonathan. He glanced up as he stuck out his hand. "Nice to meet you," he said.

Jonathan shook his hand. "Likewise. And congrats on the wedding."

Rob nodded. "Thanks."

Silence engulfed them, so Jonathan glanced over at Stacy, who was just holding onto Rob's arm and smiling up at him.

"I think I'll take Jonathan to get some food," Tiffany said. The sensation of her arm on his caused his skin to warm.

It was shocking and soothing at the same time. Glancing down, he saw Tiffany peek up at him. As if she, too, were unsure if touching him was okay.

"Yes, of course. Get some food. We've got rounds to make," Stacy said as she tugged on Rob's arm again. Then, just before she disappeared into the crowd of people, she turned around. "Meet up after lunch. We've got things to do, wedding party!"

Jonathan chuckled as they made their way through the crowd. But, when Tiffany didn't drop her arm, his chuckle died down. Glancing at her hand as it rested on his forearm, he couldn't help but feel calm. Like being this close to her was exactly what he was made to do.

They made their way to the end of the line, Tiffany nodding and hugging people along the way. Jonathan just followed her, keeping quiet as she reconnected with members of her family.

When they got to the food, Tiffany dropped her arm to pick up a plate. Jonathan's arm grew cold from the absence of her touch. Feeling like an idiot, he grabbed a plate as well and focused on filling it.

When they got to their table, they kept the conversation light. Jonathan asked about the different members of her family. Tiffany told stories about herself as a kid. It was nice to sit and talk, but Jonathan couldn't help but feel like something was missing. Something between them had changed, and as much as he didn't want to find out what it was, he knew they would eventually have to figure it out.

He wasn't sure how their relationship would change; he just knew it would.

Two hours later, Jonathan was standing on the pedestal at the tux rental place as a man with a thick Italian accent circled around him. The man had pins pinched between his lips and his eyes were squinted.

Thankfully, Rob had convinced the man to work with an existing tux so that Jonathan's would be ready by tomorrow. But Jonathan could tell from the man's deep sighs that he was not happy with the short amount of time he'd been given.

Rob was standing next to his other groomsmen, talking. Feeling like an idiot for taking so long, Jonathan tried to get the man to speed up. But there seemed to be a language barrier between them because the man just muttered something in Italian and continued pinning.

Rob's phone rang, and he pulled it from his pocket. He swiped it on and pressed it to his ear. After a minute, he whooped and then turned, announcing that Trent was coming. The other men seemed to know who that was because they shouted as well.

Their enthusiasm caused Jonathan to smile, even though he had no idea who Trent was. Then, Rob's gaze fell onto Jonathan and his expression grew serious. He tipped the phone back to his lips.

"You know Tiffany and Beatrice are here," Rob said.

Confused, Jonathan studied him. And then realization dawned on him. He remembered Tiffany saying something about a regret named Trent, but he wasn't sure if it was the same guy.

Rob focused his gaze on the ground and then nodded a few times. "Right. Well, Tiffany has a date here too. I'm sure you two will be fine."

Worry crept up into Jonathan's stomach as he leaned forward to listen to what Rob was saying. Even though he was trying to act as if it didn't matter, Jonathan couldn't help but feel that Tiffany was about to have a major surprise.

Rob said goodbye and then hung up the phone. He glanced over at Jonathan and gave him a smile.

Jonathan furrowed his brow. "Who's Trent?"

Rob shrugged. "An old friend," he said. Just as he passed by Jonathan, he turned. "He's actually Tiffany's ex from a few years back. Something happened between him and Beatrice." He shook his head. "A whole lot of drama you don't want get into. But she's dating you now, so everything should be good." He gave Jonathan a wide smile as he joined the other guys.

From what Jonathan could pick out of their conversation, they were talking about which bar to go to for the bachelor party, but Jonathan really wasn't listening. Instead, he was standing on the stupid pedestal, wishing his phone wasn't in his pants that were hanging from the chair.

He needed to warn Tiffany before it was too late.

CHAPTER EIGHT

Tiffany sat on the cream-colored couch, sipping some champagne as Stacy twirled in front of her. She was wearing her wedding dress and fluffing her veil around her face.

Georgina, Beatrice, and Heather were standing next to her, exclaiming how beautiful she looked. She did look beautiful, but Tiffany really wasn't in the mood to dote on her. She was still trying to wrap her head around what had happened with Jonathan outside the elevator after running into Beatrice on the way down for lunch.

He'd wrapped his arm around her and brought her next to him like she was his. Not like she was his friend. But *his*.

Shivers rushed across her skin as she pushed that thought from her mind. Had she gone mental? Jonathan was not a romantic interest for her. He was her friend. That was all.

Her. Friend.

"So tell us about Jonathan," Heather said, turning to wink at Tiffany.

Tiffany had been mid-sip and inhaled a bit of champagne. Her eyes watered as she stifled the cough in her throat. "He's, um..." She coughed a few times as she tried to figure out how to label him. "He's the best guy a girl could ask for."

"Then why is he with you?" Beatrice whispered as she passed by Tiffany.

Tiffany glared at her. The history between them was never going to die. It'd been a mistake, one that Tiffany wished she could take back. But she couldn't, and Beatrice seemed set on hating Tiffany forever.

Deciding to ignore her, Tiffany glanced over at Heather, who was smiling—oblivious to the interchange between Tiffany and Beatrice. "He is a hottie, girl. Man, does he have brothers?"

Tiffany chuckled as she nodded. "Four actually." She could hear Mrs. Braxton lamenting the single status of her sons. Tiffany was sure a wedding like this was exactly what Mrs. Braxton would use to change that.

Heather fanned her face. "Are they coming?" she asked with a giggle.

Tiffany furrowed her brow as she shook her head. "No. One's dating my best friend, and the other two aren't in South Carolina."

Heather stuck out her bottom lip as she collapsed on the couch. "I've got the worst luck," she said, folding her arms. "You've got a hot NFL player on your arm, and I've got Teddy, my dad's accountant."

Tiffany laughed. "Really? Your dad's accountant?"

Heather picked up a pillow and chucked it at Tiffany. "Hey, he's not that old."

Tiffany caught the pillow and threw it back. "But is he young?"

Heather paused and then a giggle erupted. "You're right. You've got me. But it's better than coming to this shindig single." Raising one hand next to her cheek to hide her gesture, she pointed toward Beatrice with her finger.

Tiffany flicked her gaze over to Beatrice and then back to Heather. She felt bad for her cousin. This was not a topic she liked discussing. Especially when she had a hand in what had happened.

Regret and sadness washed over her as she mustered a smile for Heather and then stood, making her way over to Stacy.

"You look beautiful," she said, wrapping her arms around her cousin and giving her a squeeze.

Stacy laughed as she pulled back. "Well, thanks for coming." Then she leaned in. "Is everything good between you and Beatrice?"

Tiffany shrugged. "We'll make it work."

Stacy pulled back to study her. Then she nodded. "Good. Cause I'm ready for my cousins to start talking to each other again."

Tiffany nodded. "Of course."

Stacy turned to the other girls and clapped her hands. "All right, I think Deb is finished with the last-minute fittings, so we are out of here in five."

They cheered as Tiffany helped Stacy off the pedestal and into the dressing room to take off the dress.

Thirty minutes later, Tiffany was following Stacy and the other bridesmaids across the parking lot of Hotel Debonaire. When they got to the front doors, they slid open, revealing the hotel lobby.

Just as Tiffany was hit with the wave of air-conditioning, her stomach dropped.

There, standing next to the check-in desk, was Trent. Someone must have not noticed that she had stopped, because they plowed right into her.

"Hey," Beatrice said, but then whatever else she was going say never came.

Turning, Tiffany studied her cousin, whose expression seemed to mirror exactly how she felt.

"What is he doing here?" Beatrice asked, whipping around to glare at Tiffany.

Tiffany held up her hands. "I didn't invite him. How could I? I haven't talked to him since..."

When the pained expression passed over Beatrice's face, Tiffany decided that mentioning that night probably wasn't the best idea, especially if she wanted her cousin to forgive her.

"Stacy," Beatrice called out as she made her way over to the bride-to-be.

Trying not to look conspicuous, Tiffany headed over to the water cooler sitting along the far wall and grabbed a cup. After filling it, she took a long drink. Just as she turned, a familiar voice stopped her.

"Hey. Fancy meeting you here."

Trent.

Turning, Tiffany gave him a quick smile. "Hey, Trent." Then, realizing how close he was, she took a step back. "What are you doing here?"

Trent's hair was blonder now. He had it styled in a way that looked like he wasn't trying—even though he obliviously was. His blue eyes danced in a flirty way that made her stomach twist.

This was not good.

"Hey, I can be here. I'm friends with Rob." He leaned in. "Unless you forgot that."

Tiffany glanced over at Beatrice, who was watching them with her lips pinched and a pained expression on her face. Worried their interaction was giving her the wrong message,

Tiffany stepped back and held her hand up to stop him from advancing.

Trent raised his eyebrows as he too flicked his gaze over to Beatrice and then back to Tiffany. "That's over and you know it. It's not my fault that she never got the memo." Then he leaned closer. "I've missed you."

Tiffany's stomach twisted. This was not the conversation she wanted to be having. Especially not about her cousin who she wanted to fix her relationship with.

Just as she opened her mouth to speak, a warm arm wrapped around her waist and pulled her next to a very warm and very muscular body.

Jonathan.

And from the look on Trent's face, he was just as startled as she was.

"Hey, babe," Jonathan said as he pressed his lips to the top of her head. "Miss me?" His fingers fiddled with her dress and sent shivers down her spine.

"Hey. Name's Trent," Trent said, reaching his hand out for Jonathan to shake.

"Jonathan."

They shook hands but remained quiet. Like they were sizing each other up.

"Here with Tiffany?" Trent asked after he finally dropped Jonathan's hand.

"Yep. She brought me here to show me off."

Tiffany laughed as she turned and pressed her hand to his chest. "You know me," she said as she glanced sideways at Trent.

Trent was watching the two of them for a moment before he pushed his hands through his hair. "Got it. Well, it was good catching up with you," Trent said, reaching out and resting his hand on her arm.

Tiffany pulled her arm away and nodded. "You too."

Trent gave her one last look before making his way over to the elevator and pressing the up button. Once he was out of range, Tiffany let out the breath she'd been holding and turned to study Jonathan—who she had just realized was still holding onto her.

She patted his hand, letting him know he could let go of her, and then glanced up at him. It took a moment for Jonathan to drop his arm. When he did, he shoved both hands into his front pockets and turned to look at her. His eyebrow was raised, and he ran his gaze over her.

"So, that was Trent."

Tiffany nodded. "That was Trent."

Jonathan leaned forward. "Are we going to talk about Trent?"

Tiffany held onto the strap of her purse like it was a lifeline. "Nope."

That seemed to surprise Jonathan. But Tiffany didn't care. There was no way she could delve into her past with him. Not right now.

Just as she boarded the elevator to head up to the room, Jonathan stuck his hand out to stop the doors and then stepped on. His inquisitive look irritated her. He didn't have to say anything. She knew he was never going to let her off that easy.

Eventually, she was going to have to tell him the truth.

They rode in silence up to the third floor, and, just as the doors opened, Tiffany hurried out.

Jonathan kept pace with her as she walked down the hall to their room. She swiped her card over the door's sensor, only for the light to remain red. Tiffany let out a frustrated groan.

A warm hand engulfed her as Jonathan stilled her movement.

"Let me," he said, his voice low and teasing.

Tiffany tried to not let it bother her. He didn't mean anything by it. He wasn't her doting boyfriend. He was just playing a part.

Turning back to the door, he swiped his card over the lock—which of course turned green right away—and pushed open the door, waving her inside.

"After you," he said, winking as she moved past him.

Tiffany went over to the bed and collapsed on it. She sighed as she flopped onto her back. All sorts of emotions were rushing through her.

The bed shifted, signaling that Jonathan had joined her. Turning her head to the side, she studied him. When he met her gaze, he gave her a relaxed smile.

How could he be so calm about this?

"Do you really need to know?" she asked, flipping to her side and bending her arm so she could rest her head on her hand.

Jonathan shrugged. "No. But we haven't really been the kind of friends who keep secrets from each other. Remember the pact?" He raised his pinkie finger and hooked it just as they had done pretty much their whole lives.

A feeling of sadness formed in the pit of her stomach as his words sank in. He was right. They'd always shared everything with each other. No matter what.

Why were things changing?

Before she allowed herself to delve into that thought, she pushed herself up and grabbed a pillow, hugging it as she sat on the bed.

"There's not a lot to tell. Five years ago, Beatrice was dating Trent. And then she wasn't, because I was." Ugh. Just saying the words out loud made her sound like a terrible person.

Who did that to their family?

Jonathan was studying her. "Really? You stole her boyfriend? Why didn't you ever tell me this?"

"I was too embarrassed. I didn't want you to think bad of me." Tiffany buried her face into the pillow. "What I did was awful," she said softly, her voice muffled.

Jonathan tsked, drawing her attention up. He was studying her with a playful smile on his lips. "Such a player," he said.

Frustrated, Tiffany grabbed the edge of the pillow and smacked him across the chest with it. "I am not. And, besides, he's a jerk. I was just helping Beatrice out. Revealing his tendencies before she got sucked in further."

Jonathan faked a hurt expression, but then he grabbed the pillow just as Tiffany went to whack him again.

He inhaled through his wide smile. "See, now that's exactly what a player would say."

"Oh!" she yelled as she launched herself forward and grabbed onto his shoulders. She shifted, trying to pull him down onto the bed, but Jonathan barely moved.

He laughed as he stared down at her. "What are you doing?" he asked.

Tiffany's face heated as she glared at him. "I'm trying to wrestle you," she said, hoping he felt the sheer weight of her menacing stare.

Jonathan quirked an eyebrow, and then he whipped his back down onto the bed, causing Tiffany to tumble on top of him.

He chuckled as he lay there, staring up at her. "You're so strong," he teased.

Frustrated, Tiffany pulled herself up and began tickling him. He twitched but remained calm.

Tiffany let out a growl as she sat up, sitting next to him. "You're no fun anymore. I can't compete against all of that." She waved at his muscles.

Jonathan sat up, glancing down to where she gestured. He flexed as he brought his gaze back up to her. "All of this?"

Rolling her eyes, she nodded. "Yes."

Jonathan leaned forward. "You better be careful. With all this talk about my body, I'm going to start getting a body complex."

Tiffany snorted. "You? A complex? Not likely." She grabbed the nearby pillow and flung it at him.

He caught it—of course—and peered over it at her. Then he threw it to the side and lunged at her. After pinning her down on the bed, he brought up her arm and dangled his fingers above her armpit.

Tiffany let out a squeal as she twisted, trying to free her hand so she could tickle him instead. But it was in vain. Jonathan weighed too much.

Then, he lowered his fingers and began to tickle her. Tiffany giggled and twisted.

"Okay, okay!" she squealed. "You win."

Jonathan wiggled his eyebrows as he stared down at her. "I win?"

She let out her breath as she met his gaze. It wasn't until that moment that she realized how close they were. He was just a foot away from her, staring down at her with his dark, intense eyes.

Suddenly, his expression stilled as he reached up and tucked a curl behind her ear. A shiver rushed across her body as his fingers brushed her skin. He studied her and she could see the gold flecks in his eyes.

Had he always had them? Why hadn't she ever noticed?

Just as he parted his lips to speak, Tiffany's phone rang, snapping her out of the trance she was in.

Suddenly needing to get as far away from him as she could, she patted his arm. He snapped back, flopping down on the bed as Tiffany got up and crossed the room to grab her phone from her purse.

"Hello?" she asked after she pressed the talk button.

"Tiff?"

"Stacy?"

"Yeah. A bunch of us are going down to the pool to hang out. Want to join us? You and Jonathan?"

Tiffany's gaze made its way over to Jonathan, who was lying there with his eyes closed. Her heart picked up speed as she studied his features. Then, feeling like an idiot, she nodded. "Yeah, sure. We can join you guys. Be down in a few minutes."

Stacy squealed her response, and a moment later, the call ended.

Tiffany sighed as she slipped her phone back into her purse. "I guess we're going to a wedding party pool shindig," she said.

Jonathan glanced over at her. "Pool party?"

Tiffany grabbed her black swimsuit out of her luggage and nodded. "Yep. So get changed."

Jonathan pulled himself up and nodded. "Perfect. I could use some time in the water."

Tiffany just smiled as she made her way into the bathroom and shut the door. Once there was a wall between her and Jonathan, her heart finally decided to calm down and return to a normal rhythm.

Sighing, she slipped on her suit and stared at herself in the mirror. She couldn't be this discombobulated. Not when she was about to face Trent. She needed her wits about her, so her confusing feelings for Jonathan were not something she should be focusing on.

If only her body could agree with her mind, then she might actually survive this weekend.

CHAPTER NINE

Jonathan stood in the hotel room in his swim trunks and flip flops. The idea of swimming had lightened his mood after the confusion he'd felt on the bed. Why had he tickled Tiffany?

Why had he allowed himself to get so close to her?

It had been a stupid move.

He cleared his throat as he pushed his hands through his hair. He needed to stop these ridiculous feelings that crept up every time he was around her.

She was his best friend. That was it. If he allowed himself to acknowledge how he was feeling, he would ruin that friendship. And he couldn't do that.

Frustrated with himself, Jonathan made his way over to the window and stared down at the pool. He could make out Stacy, Rob, and the rest of the wedding party down there.

Feeling anxious to get going, he turned to call out Tiffany's name. But nothing escaped his lips. Everything came to a halt when he saw her.

She was standing there in a black swimsuit. It hugged her curves and hinted to the womanly figure underneath. She was pulling her hair up into a ponytail, exposing the length of her neck.

Realizing that he was staring, Jonathan dropped his gaze. After she finished putting her hair up, she grabbed a swimsuit cover and then glanced over at him.

"Ready?" she asked. Thankfully, not addressing the fact that he'd just been checking her out.

Good. That was the last thing he needed.

Worried how his voice would come out, Jonathan just nodded.

Tiffany threw a towel to him, which he caught and draped over his neck. Then he followed her out of the room and over to the elevator.

Tiffany filled the silence by recounting the events that took place during the final dress fitting earlier that day. Jonathan just stood there, listening to what she was saying and trying hard not to let his thoughts wander.

Which was tougher when she laughed and her nose crinkled. Or when her cheeks flushed from embarrassment.

Why hadn't he ever noticed how beautiful she was? Or the way her dark hair accented her pale skin. Or how the light dusting of freckles across her nose made him want to run his fingers over them.

Whoa. Control your thoughts, Braxton, he scolded himself.

The last thing he needed was to find himself doing in real life any of things he was imagining in his mind.

That would make for an awkward conversation.

Thankfully, the doors to the elevator opened and Tiffany stepped out, not missing a beat as she continued her narration. Jonathan kept a reasonable distance from her as he listened to her story.

When they got outside, the wedding party cheered as they engulfed them. A few of the guys pounded Jonathan on the back, but he wasn't really paying attention. Instead, he kept his gaze on Tiffany, who'd made her way over to the bar while talking to Heather.

"Geez, man," Rob said as he walked up to Jonathan. He wore sunglasses and had a beer in his hand. "I need to know your regimen." He waved at Jonathan's chest.

Jonathan shrugged as he made his way to the bar as well. "It's not much, man. Just lifting and a lean diet."

Rob scoffed. "Yeah, right."

Jonathan gave him a smile as he stepped up next to Tiffany. She glanced over at him.

"Miss me already?" She asked in a flirty tone. He wasn't sure what to read into it so decided not to.

Jonathan shook his head. "Nope. Just thirsty."

Tiffany laughed. "Right."

Jonathan grabbed his sunglasses from his pocket and slipped them on as he ordered a beer. Then he turned, resting his arms on the bar. "I'm actually glad to get a break." He glanced over at her and smiled. "You talk too much."

Tiffany dropped her jaw. "I do not," she said as she poked him in the ribs.

Jonathan shrugged. "Well, that's your opinion."

"What's your opinion?" a deep voice asked, drawing Jonathan's attention over to Trent, who was standing next to Tiffany with a wide smile on his lips.

Tiffany shrugged. "Nothing. Never mind." The bartender brought her glass of wine and she took it from him and turned. She gave Jonathan a panicked look and then walked away.

Now alone with Trent, Jonathan glanced over at him. The strange urge to punch the guy rose up in his stomach.

"Good to see you again," he said, reaching his hand over. He needed to do something before he acted on the feelings inside of him.

Trent glanced down at his hand and then took it. "Likewise."

They shook for a moment before Jonathan dropped his hand. He reached over and grabbed his beer and took a long drink from it. When he was done, he glanced over at Trent, who was still standing there.

"So, how do you know the bride and groom?"

Trent's beer arrived, and then he turned to face Jonathan. "We go way back. In fact, a lot of us go way back." A knowing smile spread across Trent's lips.

Jonathan cleared his throat as he pushed down the frustration that was rising in his chest. There was no reason to act rash. At least, not yet.

"Well, some things are best left in the past," he said as his gaze made its way over to Tiffany. She was standing next to the pool, talking to Stacy. Her smile was infectious, causing Jonathan to smile as well.

"And you?" Trent asked.

Jonathan glanced over at him. "What?"

"How do you know the bride and groom."

Jonathan took another drink. "I don't. I'm here with Tiffany. Unless you didn't know that."

Trent shrugged. "Doesn't bother me much."

"Oh really?"

Trent glanced over at Jonathan. "Why? Does she talk about me?"

Jonathan straightened. There was no way he wanted to let this jerk know that Tiffany wasted any of her breath on him. He shrugged. "You may have come up once. When we were listing the greatest mistakes we've ever made." He grinned over at Trent as he pushed away from the bar and headed over to Tiffany.

Before he talked himself out of it, he wrapped his arms around her waist from behind and pulled her against him.

Tipping his lips toward her ear, he whispered, "Just go along with it."

Tiffany had tensed at first, and then, as his words registered, she relaxed. "What's going on?" she asked.

His skin tingled when she brought up her hand to rest it on his arms. His whole body heated from the intimacy they were sharing. And the fact that it was in front of all these people made it…real.

Shaking off those thoughts, he spun her around until she was facing him. Then he wrapped his arms around her waist and pulled her up until she was level with him.

Her eyes widened as—for a second—her gaze dropped down to his lips. His heart hammered in his chest as he thought about what that meant. Did she…?

Idiot. Don't even go there.

"Just making certain people jealous," he said as he lowered her to the ground and then dipped forward to kiss her forehead.

"Certain people?" she breathed as her hands remained resting on his chest. They felt as if they were on fire from the way his body was reacting.

Jonathan almost lost himself in how it felt to leave a trail of kisses from her forehead, down to her temple, until he reached her ear. Then, he forced himself to focus on her question. "Trent," he whispered.

She tensed at the name, and he felt her turn her head as if she were searching for the guy. Not wanting to ruin this moment, he brought up his finger to her chin and gently turned her face back until her gaze met his.

"I've got this covered," he said. He held her gaze as if he needed her to know that he'd always take care of her.

That was his job.

Tiffany studied him, her expression softening. She parted her lips, but nothing came out.

Allowing himself to throw caution to the wind, he let his gaze dip down to study her perfect lips. It wasn't until now that he noticed how full they were. Or how completely kissable they seemed.

When he returned his gaze to hers, he saw confusion there. As if she too was trying to figure out what was happening.

Was something happening?

A hand landed on Jonathan's back, breaking the hold Tiffany seemed to have on him. Glancing over, he saw Rob standing there.

"Don't mean to interrupt, but we are starting a game of chicken. You guys in?"

Jonathan glanced over at Tiffany. She'd stepped back and was adjusting her ponytail as if they hadn't just experienced a very intense and very confusing moment together.

"I'm in," he said.

Tiffany pinched her lips together and nodded.

Rob whooped and pumped his fists in the air. "Awesome. Jonathan, you're with Beatrice and Tiffany..." Rob glanced around. Jonathan stared at him, trying to process what was happening.

Before Jonathan could ask, Rob said, "You're with Trent."

Jonathan finally found his voice as he reached out to grab Rob's arm. "What? Why?"

Rob glanced over at him. "You can't be on the same team as your significant other. It's more fun this way." Rob patted Jonathan on the shoulder while he winked. "You'll be fine. Beatrice is light."

Jonathan glanced over at Tiffany, who looked just as shocked as he felt. Was it too late to back out now?

"Hey, Jonathan," Beatrice's soft voice drew his attention over.

He nodded. "Hey."

"This really is ridiculous. But I'm excited to be your partner."

Jonathan nodded again, not sure how to interpret any of this. He couldn't help but glance over at Tiffany, who was standing there like someone had slapped her in the face. It didn't take long for Trent to saunter over to her and lean in.

He said something to her, but Jonathan couldn't hear what. He strained to make out their words, but Beatrice was talking too loud.

Realizing that it was in vain, Jonathan gave Tiffany an encouraging smile and then glanced down at Beatrice. She'd finished talking, but Jonathan couldn't remember what she'd said.

So all he could do was nod. When she didn't react right away, he wondered if he'd made a mistake. But from the smile that finally emerged, he'd done something right—if only he knew what that was.

"Alright, first set of couples, into the pool," Rob yelled out, raising his hand and motioning toward Jonathan, Beatrice, Tiffany, and Trent.

Jonathan nodded and cannonballed into the water. Beatrice was a bit daintier, slipping into the water from the edge of the pool. Jonathan wiped the droplets from his face and hair as he watched her walk carefully over to him. He studied her, not sure how he was going to get her up onto his shoulders without the chance of touching her somewhere he really didn't want to.

Beatrice gave him a smile and then motioned toward the water. "Bend down maybe?" she asked.

Nodding, Jonathan sank down to his knees and turned so his back was to her. He felt the pressure of her hands on his shoulders. He bent down farther until her leg appeared in his peripheral. He helped hold her steady as she brought up the other leg.

He almost dumped her back into the water, but he caught her in time. His heart was pounding, but he finally straightened with her on his shoulders.

He waited in the middle of the pool for Tiffany to get situated on Trent's shoulders. Her lips were pinched as she held her hands out. Trent was saying something to her, but Tiffany didn't look like she appreciated what he was saying—or perhaps she just didn't appreciate that he was talking to her at all.

Rob didn't seem to pick up on her cool reaction to Trent. Instead, he clapped his hands and announced that it was time for the contestants to get ready.

Jonathan and Trent walked toward the center of the pool. They stood a few feet apart as Rob explained that there would be no cheating or eye gouging. Then he started to count down from three.

"Go!" he shouted.

Jonathan held onto Beatrice's thighs, hoping that he could keep her steady enough to stay upright. It was taking all of his muscle and brain power to keep from slipping. Tiffany was strong, and it was showing in the way Beatrice rocked back and forth.

Cheers rose up around them when Trent slipped and almost took both of them down. But at the last minute, he caught himself and straightened up.

Just when Jonathan thought his legs were going to give out, a splash sounded. Tiffany was down.

Jonathan whooped and helped Beatrice slip off his shoulders and into the water. Tiffany had yet to surface. Worried something was the matter, he walked through the water over to where he could see her floating.

He was inches away from her when she popped back up. She pushed her hair from her face and then twitched as if she hadn't expected him to be there.

"You okay?" Jonathan asked, reaching out to rest his hand on her shoulder.

Tiffany's gaze dropped down to his hand and then back up to him.

"Yeah. I'm fine," she said. Her voice was flat and definitely didn't sound fine.

Had he done something wrong? Jonathan dipped down so that she would have to look at him. "You sure?"

Tiffany rubbed her forehead. "Yep. Totally fine. I don't always need to be rescued."

Jonathan studied her. The bite to her tone surprised him as much as her actual words did. "I really didn't want to—"

"I said I'm okay," Tiffany said as she pulled away from him and began walking through the water in the direction of the ladder.

A few seconds later, she was pulling herself out, and Jonathan couldn't help but watch her. Something was up. She was definitely not being honest with him.

"She okay?" Trent asked.

Turning, Jonathan saw Trent standing next to him. He had a slight smile on his lips. Jonathan wondered if Tiffany's sudden coolness had anything to do with him.

"Yeah. She's fine." Then Jonathan turned so Trent could feel the whole weight of his words. "Did you say anything to her?"

Trent placed his hand on his chest. "Me? What would I say?" Then he gave Jonathan a wink and pushed back against the water until he was floating on his back.

Jonathan wanted to follow after the guy and demand to know what he did to Tiffany, but Trent wasn't worth it. Besides, he doubted that it would win him any points with Tiffany—who had wrapped a towel around her waist and was standing at the bar.

"We made quite a team," Beatrice's quiet voice drew

Jonathan's attention.

She was smiling up at him and her hair was glistening in the sunlight. She was really beautiful. Her smile melted his frustration a bit. Just because Tiffany was struggling with people here, didn't mean he had to. Besides, Tiffany was being confusing, and Beatrice was sweet.

"We did, didn't we," Jonathan said, winking at her. "If they ever recognize this as a sport, we should try out for the Olympics."

Beatrice giggled as she reached out and rested her hand on his arm. "We should. We'd definitely get the gold."

"Oh, definitely."

Beatrice held his arm for a moment before she reached up to squeeze out her hair. Then she glanced over at him. "Do you want to get a drink sometime? I mean, while you're here?"

Jonathan's stomach sank as his gaze flicked to Tiffany. She was watching them, but as soon as his gaze met hers, she turned her attention to the bartender. Her laughter was so loud that it could be heard where Jonathan was standing.

"I mean, just as victors. Not as a date." Beatrice leaned in and gave him a soft smile. "I know you're with Tiffany."

Jonathan glanced down at her and then back over at Tiffany. When she didn't look back, he shrugged off the way she was acting. They weren't really dating, so what was the harm? Plus, Tiffany knew he was looking for someone. They'd talked about it before they got here.

It was just one drink. And going out with another woman might help him sort out the strange feelings that were growing inside of him. Feelings for Tiffany that he knew he was not supposed to be feeling.

At all.

So he gave Beatrice his best heart-stopping smile and nodded. "Sure."

CHAPTER TEN

The bartender was saying something to Tiffany, but she couldn't really understand. She wasn't really listening. Trent whispering after the fight that she was never good at anything, plus seeing Jonathan talking to Beatrice, had put her in a foul mood. And as a result, she decided to strike up a conversation with Cody—the bartender—but he wasn't really her type.

Well, with the way she was feeling about Jonathan, she wasn't sure what her type was anymore. Cody seemed sweet. He was tall, with thick blond hair and a smile that spread across his face.

"I get off at seven," Cody said, drawing her attention back to him.

His words didn't quite register, so she leaned forward. "I'm sorry, what?"

Cody smiled, his blond hair falling into his eyes. He tipped his head and gave her a wink. She studied him. She didn't want to go out with Cody. She didn't even want to talk to him. But with her emotions the way they were right now, she wasn't really in the right mindset to make a decision.

So she just smiled and took the margarita from him and sipped on it for a moment.

Cody jotted something down on a napkin and then pushed it over to her. "Think about it," he said as he gave her a flirty smile and then headed over to take a rather plump woman's order.

Tiffany nodded and crumpled the napkin up in her hand. She drank her margarita so fast she gave herself a brain freeze, but she wanted to be done before Cody returned. Leaving her glass on the bar, she turned and almost ran face-first into Jonathan's chest.

She yelped as she pulled back. Glancing up, she saw him staring down at her with a very confused look on his face.

"What was that about?" he asked, reaching over and curling his fingers around her clasped hand.

She shifted and stepped to the side, hoping to deter any further questions.

Jonathan just tightened his grasp on her hand and pulled her next to him. He wrapped his arm around her waist and dipped down until his lips barely touched her ear.

Shivers rushed over her skin as warmth erupted inside of her. She closed her eyes for a moment, reveling in the feeling of his body pressed against hers. Why was she reacting like this? Didn't her body know that he was her friend? That their relationship wasn't real?

If she allowed herself to feel the way she so desperately wanted to feel, she'd ruin the only relationship she'd been able to keep. And then she was just perpetuating her past. She always destroyed relationships with people she cared about. They left. They always did.

Trent had been right. She was an utter failure, and she was only going to continue failing. Jonathan wasn't immune to her inadequacies.

No matter how much she wanted things to change.

"Why are you getting the bartender's number?" Jonathan's breath was warm against her skin, and the tone of his voice was one of worry, not accusation. "Do I suck that much at being your fake boyfriend?"

Tiffany pulled back so she could meet his gaze. She hated that he was confused because of her weakness. She couldn't tell him how she felt, though. There really was no coming back from something like that.

"It's not you," she said, giving him a small smile.

He quirked an eyebrow. "Really? Isn't that what you say when you're going to break up with someone? It's not you, it's me?"

She chewed her lip and nodded. "But I mean it. This"—she waved at herself—"is a mess. You don't want to be a part of this mess."

Jonathan furrowed his brow as he studied her. "What are you talking about? You're a mess?" He pulled her closer. "Tiff, you forget that I know you. I'm not scared."

Her stomach lightened as she forced herself to meet his gaze. He held it with an intensity that almost took her breath away. She wanted to believe that was true. That, perhaps, he knew her enough to accept her. All of her.

But he didn't really know her. And if he found out, he'd run. He was her best friend, but that didn't mean he had to stick around.

So she forced a smile. "I'm fine. I'm just tired. It's been a long day." She patted his chest and then pushed off him. Jonathan hesitated but finally dropped his arms.

He pushed his hands through his wet hair, causing it to stand up. He looked adorable and unkempt, and she couldn't help but hold her breath as he glanced around.

Why, oh why, did she have to start getting feelings for her best friend? Was she an idiot? She ruined every relationship she'd ever gotten into. She couldn't do it to this one.

Jonathan finally brought his attention back to her. He looked uncertain. "So what now? Do you want to get back into the pool?"

Rob was cheering as two more couples were battling each other in a game of chicken. She wasn't interested in climbing back onto Trent's shoulders, and she certainly did not want to get on Jonathan's. She shrugged. "I could use a shower and a nap."

Jonathan sighed. "Okay. I guess I can hang out here."

Tiffany turned and started to head toward the hotel's doors. But the feeling of Jonathan wrapping his hand around her elbow stopped her. She glanced over her shoulder as he stepped up next to her.

"I just want you to be happy, Tiff. If you need to call off our fake relationship to chase that happiness, I'll back down."

Tiffany winced as his words washed over her. She really was an awful friend. Who drags their best friend to a wedding, asks them to fake a relationship, and then ditches them when things got hard?

Calling off their fake relationship was the last thing she wanted to do, but maybe it was for the best.

"Is that what you want?" she asked, focusing her gaze on the water. There was no way she could look at him right now. Not when his answer might break her heart.

When he didn't respond, she peeked up at him, only to see him studying her. His gaze was intense and it took her breath away.

Stupid emotions. Why was she reading into everything he did? She doubted he had anything but platonic feelings for her.

"Jonathan?" she asked, not sure she could handle waiting for him to respond.

"I'm still game if you are."

Relief flooded over Tiffany as she nodded. "I'm game."

Jonathan's half-smile emerged as he leaned in. "But if you want that to change, you'll let me know, right? I won't hold our fake relationship over you."

Tiffany nodded. She needed to get out of here before she said the wrong thing. Before she told him that she wanted things to change but not in the direction he thought.

"I'm going to go," she said as she stepped forward, breaking their connection.

Jonathan seemed to get the picture and dropped his hand, letting her leave without any other questions.

Tiffany hurried from the pool and into the hotel. Once she got to the room, she turned on the shower and peeled off her bathing suit. Once she was under the water, she took a few deep breaths.

What was wrong with her? Why was fate so cruel?

She shouldn't be having feelings for her best friend. Of course, it was only a matter of time before she ruined their relationship. But now that feelings were involved, they were on a one-way trip to break-up-ville, where she was Mayor.

"Idiot," she said under her breath as she closed her eyes and let the water cascade over her.

Only an idiot would let this happen.

A half an hour later, she turned off the water and wrapped one of the hotel's complimentary robes around her. After wrapping her hair up in a towel, she pulled open the bathroom door and glanced out.

Relieved that Jonathan hadn't come back yet, she made her way out into the room and sat on the bed. A sense of loneliness washed over her.

How was she going to move on from this? How was she going to be around him all weekend without destroying the one relationship she'd worked so hard to maintain?

Flopping back on the bed, she let out a groan. She closed

her eyes as she slowed her breathing. One thing was for sure, she couldn't freak out. Not now.

If she did, she was bound to do something stupid.

"I can do this," she whispered under her breath as she lay there with her eyes closed. "I can do this."

A sense of calm surrounded her as she forced herself to smile. If she could act like breaking up with every guy she'd ever dated didn't break her heart, then she could act like she didn't like Jonathan.

Besides, she was just being ridiculous right now. It had to be a combination of the breakup with Sean and the fact that she was at a wedding, surrounded by love.

Maybe the best thing for her to do was to let Jonathan go. He had a chance to find someone here, and maybe she did as well. That might help pull her out of the funk she was in.

The best way to get over a crush is to find a new one. So that was what she would do.

Renewed with purpose, Tiffany sat up and took a deep breath. She felt better already. When Jonathan came back to the room, she'd release him from the obligation of being her fake boyfriend and allow him to date who he wanted to.

She was headed to a bachelorette party—aka a bar—where she was sure there would be a plethora of guys to date.

It was a perfect plan.

And if she didn't find someone tonight, there was always the bartender, Cody. He might be just what she needed to fix this sudden infatuation with her best friend.

By the time Jonathan got back to the room, she'd dried her hair and was in the middle of applying her makeup.

When Jonathan walked in, his hair was dry and sticking up in every direction. His cheeks had a pink hue, and he looked...happy.

Which was good. That meant that he hadn't picked up on

her ridiculous crush. She could definitely salvage their relationship if she could just keep her feelings in check.

She quirked an eyebrow. "Have fun?"

Jonathan walked over to the mini fridge and pulled out a bottle of water. When half of it was gone, he nodded as he returned the lid. "Yeah. Your family is crazy."

"Oh really?" Tiffany said as she turned to the mirror and began applying eyeliner.

"Yeah, your aunts came down and got into the water. It was like an attack of small, very forceful women. I barely got out of there with my life." Jonathan's voice grew louder as he neared her.

Laughing, Tiffany turned to see that he was about a foot from her. His shoulder was inches from touching her own, and he was smiling at her in the mirror.

He turned to meet her gaze. "Thanks for bringing me. This was fun." He turned to fold his arms and lean against the counter. "I needed it."

Tiffany nodded as she moved to line the other eye. "I'm happy you are having fun."

Jonathan didn't say anything. When Tiffany was done, she glanced over at him. He had a contemplative look on his face as he stared at the wall in front of him.

"So I was thinking about what you said earlier," she said, starting slow. She wasn't exactly sure how she was going to handle this, but she knew she needed to say it. For both their sakes.

"About what?" He glanced over at her and gave her one of his relaxed smiles.

"About our fake relationship."

Turning to the sink, Jonathan flipped on the water and let it fill up in his hand. "Okay," he said.

"Well, a wedding is the perfect place to pick up someone."

He glanced over at her, his eyebrows furrowing. Her

confidence wavered, but then she decided to push through. She could do this. She could.

"Okay," he said again, taking the time to drag out each letter.

"So why don't we just put this whole fake relationship thing behind us and move on?" She waved to his chest. "You can date and I can date."

He turned off the water and then straightened, staring down at her. "Are you breaking up with me?"

Tiffany's heart pounded harder at the intensity of his stare, but she held her ground. This was the safest course of action. For the both of them. He needed to find someone as much as she did.

If Jonathan was off-limits, then she just might be able to conquer these feelings building up inside of her. Which she so desperately needed to do.

Just when she thought she was going to melt under his scrutiny, he shrugged and moved toward the bathroom. "I'm going to take a shower," he said.

Tiffany watched his retreat, her lips parted. She wanted to say something. To get an answer from him. She wanted him to release her from their agreement.

But he didn't.

Instead, the bathroom door shut and the shower started. Frustrated, Tiffany turned back to the mirror and stared at herself.

She was not going to let herself ruin this relationship. Jonathan was just being nice. He felt as if he needed to protect her, and she was going to tell him that was ridiculous.

She wasn't his to protect.

Before she could stop herself, she marched over to the bathroom and flung open the door. Steam had filled the room.

"Jonathan Braxton," she said in her best *you better take me seriously* voice.

The shower curtain moved, and Jonathan's head appeared next to the wall.

"What the he—"

"Why won't you break up with me?" She placed her hands on her hips and glared at him.

Jonathan's eyebrows rose as his expression softened. "Because—"

"I don't need protection. I'll be just fine. I've been fine my whole life. You don't need to shield me from anything." Her hands began to shake as the adrenaline that was coursing through her veins wore off. Not wanting him to see, she folded her arms and narrowed her gaze.

He studied her and then sighed. "Can I talk now?"

Feeling like an idiot, Tiffany nodded. "Of course."

His gaze roamed over her as he moved to lean his shoulder against the wall. "Is that what you really want?"

No.

But she couldn't say that. So she mustered the best smile she could and nodded. "Yes. I think it's best. For the both of us."

He pinched his lips together and then nodded. "Okay."

"Okay?"

He narrowed his eyes. "Why is that so surprising to you? Did you think I was getting feelings for you or something? That I thought this was real?"

Tiffany let out a forced laugh. That was definitely not what she thought was happening to *him,* but it was definitely what was happening to *her.*

"No," she said.

Jonathan studied her and then nodded. "Perfect. Then it's an amicable breakup."

"Great."

He raised his eyebrows. “Are you going to stay in here while I shower?”

Suddenly realizing that she was still standing in the bathroom with him, Tiffany’s whole body heated. “Sorry,” she said as she made her way out to the room and shut the bathroom door behind her.

Now alone, she let out of her breath. This was for the best. All of it. Jonathan was now free to go out and find the future Mrs. Braxton, and she would keep her best friend right where she needed him. Where she couldn’t ruin their relationship.

Now, if only she could get her heart to stop breaking, she just might be able to survive this.

CHAPTER ELEVEN

Jonathan stood in front of the mirror, staring at himself. His stomach was in knots, and even though he was trying to tell himself he didn't know why—he knew he did.

Tiffany's words were circling around in his mind like a headache he just couldn't kick.

She wanted to call the fake relationship off.

Why?

He shifted his attention over to Tiffany. She was sitting on the chair next to the desk, studying her phone, oblivious to the fact that he was watching her.

Her dark hair fell forward, brushing her arms as they rested in her lap. She was still wrapped up in the white hotel robe, but the rest of her looked as if she were ready for a night on the town.

Which she was.

Without him.

Flexing his jaw, Jonathan turned his attention back to the mirror. Maybe this was what he needed. A break from

Tiffany might jumpstart his emotions and get them back on track. If he didn't, he worried what he might do.

If the growing desires inside of him were let lose, he was pretty sure he was going to ruin the one relationship he'd managed to hang onto his whole life. He'd already failed at so much that he couldn't take this risk with Tiffany. She meant too much to him.

Tiffany's groan drew his attention over to her as he squirted hair gel into his hand. Her forehead was wrinkled and she looked annoyed.

"Everything okay?" he asked, hoping he sounded more casual than he felt.

Tiffany glanced up at him and nodded. "Yeah. Fine. Just found out from Stacy that the party tonight is actually a bachelor/bachelorette party. We'll be going together."

He studied her. "That's strange."

She shrugged as she set her phone down on the desk and leaned back in her chair. "Apparently, they both want to keep an eye on each other." She folded her arms over her chest and blew out her breath.

"This is bad...because?"

Her eyes widened as she turned to study him. She pinched her lips as if she were trying not to say something. He wondered what that meant. Did she really not want to go out with him?

"Because of Trent, of course."

And then he felt like an idiot. Of course she was upset about having to spend more time with the guy that had come between her and her cousin. Why was he so stupid that he thought it was about him?

"Right. I'm sorry," he said as he pushed his hair around to style it.

He could see her from the mirror as she stood and began

to pace around the room. "It's just weird, isn't it? I mean, who does these kinds of parties together?"

Jonathan shrugged. "A buddy of mine did a guy/girl baby shower. It's not that uncommon anymore."

Tiffany stopped moving to study him. "Yeah, well, I needed a night with the girls."

Ouch. His expression faltered, but he forced a smile when he looked up at her. Before, a response like that wouldn't have bothered him. But now? It felt like a knife to the gut.

"Getting sick of me already?" Jonathan asked as he turned the water on to rinse off his hands.

Tiffany's expression softened as she stepped up next to him. "Not you. Other…other people are bugging me. Sometimes, I wish I could just take a break from everything."

As much as Jonathan wanted to believe what she said was true, he couldn't help but sense something else behind her words. Something she was trying hard not to say. It confused and frustrated him.

Since when had things come to this? They were friends. They'd always been honest with each other. And yet, it didn't feel that way now. It felt as if there was a secret that neither of them could say.

"I'm sorry." He moved over to the bed and sat down. "I don't have to go if you don't want me to."

Tiffany's gaze followed him as her expression fell. "No. I want you to go." Then she sighed and forced a smile. "Don't let me be the downer here. You deserve a break too." She moved over to sit next to him. Her arm brushed his and sent shivers up his arm. It felt so right to sit next to her, their bodies touching.

He had to fight the urge to reach over and engulf her hand with his own. It was something he would have done back when his feelings weren't so confusing. It would have been as natural as breathing to him. But now? It felt too intimate, and he wasn't sure if his heart could handle it.

So he kept his hands clasped in his lap. Tiffany sighed next to him as they sat in silence. He glanced over at her to see that her shoulders were slumped. He could feel the tension around her, and in the deepest parts of his soul, he wanted to fix whatever was bothering her.

Maybe it was because she was lonely. All the idiot guys around her didn't see her for who she was. How great of a person she was. They didn't deserve her.

But that didn't mean she wasn't lonely, and it broke his heart that she was in pain. He wanted to help her, and having a solution to her problem was the way to do that.

So, despite the fact that there were warning bells going off in his mind, he wrapped his arm around her shoulders and pulled her close. "I'll help you find the perfect guy for you," he said as he leaned down and pressed his lips to the top of her head.

Tiffany stiffened but then relaxed. "What?" she whispered.

Tightening his grip on his best friend, he dipped down to meet her gaze. "I'm going to help you find the perfect guy. You deserve that kind of love." He gave her a small smile even though his heart felt as if it might break. Finding someone for Tiffany meant finding someone to take her away from him. He wasn't so delusional as to think that once she was involved with someone else, she'd still have time for him.

She wouldn't.

But that was okay. He loved Tiffany enough to let her go. To let her be happy.

Her gaze turned stormy for a moment as she studied him. Then she pinched her lips together and nodded. "If you think that's the right thing, then I'm game."

Jonathan wanted to shake his head. He wanted to tell her

that it was actually the last thing he wanted. That the thought of helping her find another man made him sick. But he couldn't. If he did tell her the things that were trying to surface inside of him, it would be a major mistake. Tiffany would never feel the same way about him. Ever.

So he mustered a smile and nodded. "Yeah, why wouldn't it be."

She held his gaze for a moment and then nodded as she pushed away from him. "I should get dressed. Stacy wants us downstairs at six. We've got dinner to grab and bars to hop." She paused and then turned to look at him. "Thanks, Jonathan. You're the best friend a girl could ask for."

Hoping to mask his wince, Jonathan just nodded. "Definitely. What are friends for?"

Her expression stilled, and then she smiled. "While we're out, we'll have to get someone for you too," she called over her shoulder as she made her way to her luggage. After she pulled out what looked like a black dress, she made her way into the bathroom and shut the door.

Now alone, Jonathan stood and made his way over to the mirror. He stared at himself as he forced down the pit that had formed in his stomach. He was stupid to let things get this far. What did he think was going to happen? That Tiffany was going to rush into his arms and proclaim her feelings for him?

He shook his head as he splashed some water on his face. He made his way over to his suitcase, where he pulled on his navy suit coat and threaded his belt through the loops on his pants. He sat down and slipped on his shoes then grabbed his wallet and keys. He wasn't sure where they were going or if he'd need to drive.

He stood and began pacing the floor of the hotel room. He needed to work off all of this pent-up energy that was causing his muscles to ache. If only he had someone to plow into, he'd feel better. That was one of the reasons he loved football so much. The physical input helped with his anxiety and stress.

Keeping his head down, he studied the carpet below his feet. Despite his efforts to still his mind, the only thing that kept coming back to him was Tiffany. Her face, her lips, her soft skin. The fact that she knew everything about him and yet still stuck around.

With her, it wasn't like a first date. It was like the twentieth date. She knew him, and he knew her. There was no mystery or questions.

Somewhere in the back of his mind, he heard the bathroom door open, and he ran right into something. Out of instinct, he reached out to grab Tiffany as she stumbled and yelped.

Realizing what he'd just done, he whipped his gaze up to see her wide eyes. She had pressed her hands to his chest and pushed back so she could study him.

Without thinking, he pulled her closer to him until her body was pressed to his. There was this deep desire in his soul that begged him to bend forward and press his lips to hers. To show her in every way possible just how much his heart was pounding. That when he was with her, he wanted her. Body and soul.

"Jonathan," she breathed. "Are you okay?"

Jonathan had to blink a few times to break the trance he was in. To push back against the feelings that were rising up inside of him. Suddenly realizing what he was doing, he cleared his throat and straightened. He pulled his arm back and put a foot of space between them.

He nodded as he shot her a sheepish look. "Sorry. I'm just a bit...distracted, that's all."

Tiffany adjusted her black dress, and Jonathan couldn't help but run his gaze over the full length of her body. The dress hugged her curves and made his heart pound. The fire that had been lit in the depths of his body only burned hotter now.

Great.

And now he was off to a bar, where he was going to attempt to hook her up with another guy.

Why had he agreed to this, again?

Oh, right. Because he was trying to be a good friend.

Tiffany adjusted her hair in the mirror and then turned to study him. "How do I look?" she asked as she turned her body for him to see every angle.

He forced down the urge to wrap a towel around her and smiled. "You look amazing," he said. The tone of his voice was deep and surprised even him. But he couldn't help it. She looked amazing, and he wanted her to know.

Her eyes were wide. "Thanks. You look great too. A lot of ladies are going to get their hearts broken tonight."

Jonathan nodded as he forced his body to calm down. Then he winked at her and shrugged. "Someone's got to do it."

Tiffany's expression tightened as she made her way over to her shoes. She sat down on the bed to slip them on, and Jonathan wondered if she did it because he'd caught her the last time she'd put them on.

But then he felt like an idiot. Why would she care if he helped hold her steady? There was no way she had the same ridiculous feelings coursing through her as he did.

Once she was finished, she grabbed her small purse and slipped it over her shoulder. She walked over to him and smiled. "Ready to go find our next love interests?"

No.

But instead of saying how he felt, he shrugged. "Oh yeah."

She nodded and made her way over to the door. He held

the door open while she passed through to the hallway. He shut the door behind him and followed her to the elevator.

A strange tension hung in the air around them as they waited for the elevator to open. Tiffany kept glancing over at him and smiling. But it wasn't her natural, carefree smile. This one was tight.

Jonathan furrowed his brow. He didn't like that she felt uncomfortable, and he suspected that it had something to do with him. He was acting weird and Tiffany was sensing it. He was ruining their relationship, and, if he didn't get his head on straight, the one girl he'd cared about his whole life would leave.

If he wanted to maintain their relationship, he needed to get his head on straight.

The doors to the elevator opened onto the lobby and everyone who was lingering there. Jonathan couldn't help but watch Tiffany as she got off the elevator and made her way over to the group of girls that was waiting for her.

Not sure what to do, Jonathan made his way over to Rob and the other groomsmen. He stood there awkwardly as the conversation flowed around him. He didn't want to be standing here. He didn't want to talk to these guys. All he wanted was to spend time with Tiffany.

But it didn't seem like that was going to happen for him.

"Ready to go, man?" Rob asked as he reached out and clapped Jonathan on the shoulder.

"Yep."

"Is it going to be okay for Tiffany to see you around other women?" Rob asked, giving him a knowing look and a wink.

"I think she'll survive. We agreed to take a break this weekend." Just as the words left his lips, Jonathan wished he could take them back.

Why was he even bringing that up? Tiffany may be okay

with them breaking off their fake arrangement, but he wasn't.

"Wow! Nice. Then you do need a party." Rob laughed as he shook Jonathan's shoulder. "I can't wait to see what the ladies at the bar do when they hear a single NFL player is in their midst."

Jonathan turned and shot Rob a smile. He hoped the guy would move the conversation forward. Just as he glanced at Rob, he noticed that Trent was leaning forward, a small smile on his lips.

Trent's gaze met Jonathan's, and he raised his eyebrows as if to signify that he'd heard their entire conversation. Then he peeled off to talk to Jordan, another groomsman.

Frustrated, Jonathan dropped his gaze as they walked through the sliding glass doors and out into the warm evening air. There was a huge stretch limo parked on the far end of the circle drive. Jonathan followed Rob over to it and slipped inside.

Once the entire wedding party was crammed into the limo, the driver shut the door and tapped the top as he walked to the driver's side.

Jonathan tried to keep his attention from slipping over to Tiffany, who was laughing at something Nick, another groomsman, had said. He tried to ignore the smiles that Trent was casting Tiffany's way. And he was trying to ignore sensation that was rising up inside of him. One that made him want to punch every guy here.

A small hand wrapped around his own, which were clenched in his lap. Startled, he glanced over to see Beatrice smiling up at him.

"Everything okay?" she asked. Her eyes were wide as she studied him.

Not sure what to do, Jonathan pulled his hand out from

under hers and adjusted his suit coat. He hoped she'd think that was the reason he needed to break their contact.

"Tiffany told us about your breakup," she said.

Instantly, Jonathan's gaze flicked over to Tiffany. She was studying him, and when their eyes met, she dropped her gaze as her cheeks flushed.

She told people they broke up? His stomach churned. Why would she do that? Then he felt like an idiot. Hadn't he done the same?

His emotions were a wreck as he wiped his palms on his pants and smiled back down at Beatrice. "It was an amicable split."

Beatrice just smiled. "Well, if you need anyone to talk to about it, I'm here. I've been told I'm a great listener."

An uneasy feeling rose up in Jonathan's stomach, but he just nodded. "I'll keep that in mind."

Beatrice nudged him with her shoulder and then turned to address the bridesmaid that was sitting next to her. Not sure where to look, Jonathan just turned his gaze down to the floor and let out his breath.

He tried to ignore the pain in his chest as he thought about Tiffany and the fact that she'd already moved on from him. He knew their relationship was fake, but for some reason, he'd allowed himself to think that she might have felt something more—like he had. But now that she was telling people they were done, he felt like a fool for hoping that she'd cared for him as more than a friend.

He was an idiot to allow himself to get in so deep. What was he going to do now?

CHAPTER TWELVE

The Lazy Bar was loud as Tiffany walked in later that evening. Things had gone somewhat well at dinner. Thankfully, Jonathan sat at a different table, so she'd been able to keep her thoughts somewhat focused on the conversation around their table.

But now, at the bar, there was less structure, which meant the likelihood of Jonathan talking to other women was going to be that much greater. And if the feelings that rose up inside of her during Jonathan and Beatrice's exchange in the limo was indicative of how she was going to react to seeing him with other girls, then this was going to be a crappy evening.

Yay for her.

Slipping onto a bar stool, she ordered a beer. The bartender grabbed a bottle and slid it over to her. She took a sip and studied the countertop. Maybe if she just stayed here with her head down, she could pretend that everything was okay.

That her heart wasn't breaking inside of her.

"Everything okay?" Trent's low voice drew her attention up.

She glanced over at him and tried hard not to roll her eyes. She pinched her lips together and turned back to the counter. This was not the conversation she wanted to have, and Trent was certainly not the person she wanted to have it with.

"I heard about your breakup," Trent said, sitting down on the stool next to her.

Her shoulders tensed at his closeness and his words. "Really? From whom?" She couldn't help herself, she needed to know if Jonathan was talking about it.

Trent waved down the bartender and order a round of shots. He glanced over at her with a small smile. "The loser who dumped you."

Tiffany's stomach soured. He was already telling people they were done. Good. That had been the plan, and she hated that it bothered her so much. Grabbing her beer, she chugged it. When it was half gone, she set the bottle back down onto the counter and turned to him.

Anger, hurt, and betrayal rose up inside of her. She knew it was ridiculous to feel that way, but she couldn't help it. It was killing her that Jonathan was this okay with her calling things off. Why wasn't he more upset?

Suddenly, Trent's hand fell on hers, and she jumped, whipping her gaze up to see him peering down at her. She furrowed her brow as she stared at him.

"Wha—"

"I was an idiot to let you go. I should have fought to keep you."

Confusion plagued her mind as she stared down at his hand and then back up at him. She wanted to process how she felt about this, but the only thing that was rushing through her mind was a bright neon sign telling her to run.

"I dumped you. End of story." She moved to pull her hand away, but Trent just held it tighter.

"It was a mistake. All of it. I should have always been with you. Beatrice was just a placeholder." He leaned closer, the smell of alcohol on his breath made the hair on the back of her neck stand up. "Why are you fighting it?"

Tiffany attempted to pull her hand away again, but Trent wouldn't relent. She glanced up at him to give him a piece of her mind, but before she could say anything, his arm was flung to the side, breaking his hold on her. She turned to see Cody, the bartender from earlier, his face contorted into a look of anger.

"What..." Her brain was trying to catch up to what was going on.

"If the lady wants to get away, you let her," Cody said as he stepped forward.

"What's the matter with you?" Trent asked as he pushed away from the counter.

Cody glanced from Tiffany to Trent. "She looked as if she wanted you to let her go. If a woman wants you to stop touching her, you stop touching her."

Trent smiled, a slow and sadistic grin. "I think we were just fine, right, Tiffany?"

Tiffany stood next to Cody as she faced Trent. "I think you should go. We're...done. Leave me alone."

Trent raised his eyebrows, and as he moved to approach her, Cody's hand shot out and squeezed Trent's shoulder. "She said you should go."

Trent glanced between them and then growled. "You're making a mistake," he said as he stomped off.

Tiffany's hands shook as she wrapped her arms around her chest and sat back on the stool. Cody joined her, sitting on Trent's now vacant one.

He glanced over at her and smiled. Not sure what to do, Tiffany let out a sigh. "Thanks for that," she said.

Cody shrugged. "I've been around my share of drunk men. I can spot a lady in distress a mile away."

Tiffany glanced over at him and nodded. "That's an awesome superpower."

Cody put his fists on his hips and straightened. "Captain Lady Saver, at your service."

"Lady Saver?"

Cody glanced down at her and then chuckled. "Yeah, kind of lame. It's the best I could come up with on such short notice."

Tiffany twisted her bottle around on the counter. She liked Cody. Maybe she shouldn't have written him off so fast. He did just come to her rescue. Maybe he was the perfect antidote to her feelings for Jonathan.

So, putting on her best flirty smile, she turned to face him. "Are you following me, or do you just frequent all the bars in search of damsels in distress."

Cody's bright blue eyes danced as he studied her. "You'd think since I'm around this stuff all the time, I'd be sick of it."

Tiffany nodded. "Yeah. Like for me, I answer phones at work. When I get home, the last thing I want to do is talk on one for fun."

Cody tapped the counter with his fingers. "Yeah. I'm not a huge drinker, so it doesn't bother me much." He waved down the bartender and ordered a Coke. "Besides, there are not a whole lot of places to meet eligible women," he said as he took the glass that the bartender had set down. He glanced at her over the rim as he took a sip.

"Eligible? Who said I was eligible?"

Cody glanced around. "I'm just guessing from the lack of guys around you and the fact that Trent was creeping. But if you're not..."

Tiffany's gaze found its way over to Jonathan, who was talking to a tall, very busty blonde. He was staring at her while she talked and flipped her hair over her shoulder. Sadness crept up inside of her as she dropped her gaze.

Get over it, Tiffany. He's moved on.

When she glanced back at Cody, she gave him a smile. "Well, you are correct. I am recently single."

Cody raised his fist and pumped the air. "Looks like it's my lucky night."

A song started up, and the crowds began to form on the dance floor. Cody stood and held out his hand. "Can I have this dance?"

Tiffany hesitated, sneaking another peek over at Jonathan. Her gaze met his, and for a moment, he held it. She wanted to interpret his expression as one of sadness, but she couldn't allow herself to hope. Instead, she pointed to Cody's back and shot Jonathan a thumbs-up.

He furrowed his brow as he pinched his lips and nodded. Even though she couldn't hear him, Tiffany could tell that he was inviting the blonde bombshell to dance. The woman squealed and grabbed his hand, dragging him to the dance floor.

Forcing her feelings to the darkest parts of her mind, Tiffany forced a smile and turned back to Cody, who had just extended his hand.

"Shall we?" he asked.

Tiffany nodded. She needed a distraction more than anything.

Cody led her out onto the dance floor. After bringing her hand up, he wrapped his arm around her waist and pulled her close.

Even though he was warm and inviting, it didn't feel quite right. Not like when Jonathan had been fake dating her. Or when he'd wrapped his arms around her and made her feel like everything was right in the world. That, with him, she could conquer anything.

Tiffany muffled a groan and mentally slapped herself. Was she serious? That's what she was thinking about while in the arms of another man?

Get a hold of yourself.

Cody began to lead her around the dance floor to some upbeat pop song. She tried to keep step with him, but it was hard with all the bodies around them.

Suddenly, she was rammed into what felt like a brick wall.

"I'm so sorry," she muttered. Then she turned to see Jonathan staring down at her.

Heat raced to her cheeks as she dropped her gaze. She could feel him still staring at her as she just stood there like an idiot.

"Hey, sorry," Cody said, reaching his hand out to shake Jonathan's.

Jonathan glanced over at Cody and then back down to Tiffany. "It's okay, man," he said, reaching over to clasp Cody's hand.

They shook for what felt like an eternity. When they finally let go, Tiffany stepped up next to Cody. "We'll try to be more careful," she muttered as she grabbed Cody's hand and silently begged for him to take her away.

Away from Jonathan who was staring down at her like she'd just abandoned him. Away from the tall blonde who was giggling and grabbing onto Jonathan's arm.

She just needed some space and time with Cody, and then her ridiculous feelings for Jonathan would go away. That was all she needed.

Time.

She half-pushed, half-danced with Cody until they were on the other side of the dance floor. Once she could no longer see Jonathan through the throng of people, she let out her breath, the stress of her feelings lessened in his absence.

Thankfully, Cody didn't seem too keen on promenading her around, so they stayed in the corner, swaying to the music. Just as the song stopped, Cody pulled away from her and smiled down. "Hey, I gotta go run to the bathroom. Wait for me?"

Tiffany wrapped her arms around her chest and nodded. "Sure."

He disappeared into the crowd as the next song—a slow one—started up. Glancing around, Tiffany made her way over to the wall and leaned against it. It was fortuitous that Cody needed a bathroom break right now. She wasn't sure how she would feel about him pulling her that close and holding her.

She closed her eyes and let the soft ballad wash over her. She began to sway a bit, relaxing as the rhythm flowed through her body. This was what she needed. She hadn't thought about Jonathan in the last minute. Which was the longest she'd gone since her feelings had decided to suddenly change on her.

"Can I have this dance?"

Shivers rushed down her body as Jonathan's deep, sexy voice washed over her. She stiffened. Great, now she was daydreaming about him. What was wrong with her?

"Tiffany?"

She peeked through her eyelashes to see Jonathan standing in front of her. He had an uneasy look on his face. When their eyes met, he pushed his hands through his hair, his shoulders slumping forward.

"Cody's in the bathroom," she blurted out.

Jonathan glanced toward the restrooms and then back to her. "Okay?"

"He'll be back," she breathed. Honestly, she wasn't sure if

she was telling Jonathan or herself. Like she'd needed to remind herself of the man who would help her forget the one standing in front of her.

"I think he'll be okay with me stealing a dance with my best friend," Jonathan said as he reached out and grabbed her hand. Tiffany wanted to pull back, to refuse him.

But as soon as the warmth of his hand met hers, it carried up her arm to her heart, and she was paralyzed. The only thing she wanted right now was to feel Jonathan next to her. To have him tell her everything was going to be okay.

She nodded.

A relieved expression passed over Jonathan's face as he pulled her off the wall and out onto the floor—all the while holding onto her hand like a lifeline.

When they got to the center of the dance floor, he turned to face her, wrapping his arm around her waist and pulling her close. Their bodies touched and Tiffany's head spun.

She swallowed as she glanced up at him. He was definitely not holding her like a guy would hold his best friend. And when she met his gaze, her breath caught in her throat. He was staring at her in an open and unabashed way. Like he wanted her to know exactly how he felt.

Fear coursed through her as she glanced down at his chest, where her other hand was resting. Every point of contact felt warm against her body.

She swallowed as they began swaying to the music. Why was she acting like such an idiot? They'd danced together before. He'd held her close before.

But right now, it felt like the first time ever. Like she was finally awake after a long sleep and Jonathan was the man who'd woken her up.

Because from the way he felt, pressed against her, he was a man. *The* man.

And she was in trouble.

"I should go find Cody," she rasped as she tried to pull back.

Jonathan's gaze dropped down to her, and he looked worried.

She didn't want him to pick up on the fact that she was literally falling for him in a way that she would only ruin, so she forced a smile. "I don't want him thinking I ditched him."

Jonathan glanced around at the crowd and then back to her. "I'm sure he'll be fine. He's survived this long without you. Besides, it's not like you've known each other for—oh. I don't know—since you were kids?"

Tiffany turned to stare at him. "Excuse me?"

Jonathan's jaw flexed as he held her gaze. "What are you doing?"

The desire to protect herself won out and she forced a shocked look. "What do you mean, what am I doing? I'm moving on from Sean. Isn't that what we agreed on?"

She stopped moving so she could focus on him. Why was he acting like this? It was sheer torture to stand there, watching Jonathan flirt with other women when all she wanted was to wrap her arms around him and kiss him.

But she was such a failure at relationships, and failing at one with Jonathan would probably kill her. That was something she could never come back from. It was for the safety of their friendship that she pulled away. She couldn't allow herself to get too wrapped up in what was happening inside of her.

Jonathan was off-limits, and she had to keep telling herself that if her heart was going to survive.

Jonathan leaned in, bringing his body inches from hers. He studied her gaze as if he were hoping to see the truth she was so desperate to hide. Her heart pounded in her chest as she held her breath.

He couldn't see her secret. It would ruin her.

"Tiffany..." he said. His hand on her back tightened, as if he thought she'd pull away—which she did want to do but couldn't find the strength.

If she was going to keep her feelings a secret, she couldn't run. If she did, he'd know.

"Yes?" Good, at least she sounded confident, even if she didn't feel that way.

His sway slowly subsided as he paused, standing there on the dance floor. He reached up and tucked her hair behind her ear. She shivered as his fingertips brushed the skin behind her ear and then ran the length of her neck.

"I, um..." He brought his gaze up to meet hers. He held it with a questioning look in his eyes.

"Jonathan," she replied, her voice barely a whisper, "I'm so happy with our friendship. It's exactly what I need. I know I can always depend on you when everything else in my life is falling apart." She needed to stop him from saying the things she was starting to suspect he felt.

If he confessed his feelings for her, she wouldn't be able to find the strength to walk away. Being with him was the only thing she really wanted. And if she got it, she'd ruin it.

She just knew it.

It was better to pretend that they couldn't be anything more than friends, than to try something she knew would fail. She couldn't lose Jonathan. Not like that.

CHAPTER THIRTEEN

Jonathan stared at Tiffany, his head swirling. He heard the words leave her lips, but they weren't registering in his brain. Like his body was literally rejecting the things she'd said.

He wasn't her friend. He couldn't be that anymore.

She was so much more to him than a friend, and he was getting tired of telling himself differently.

It was pure torture to see her flirt with Cody, and he'd tried to mask it with Shelby—the tall, blonde model—but nothing could mask the dull ache in his chest. All he wanted was Tiffany.

She was all he'd ever need. If only she'd let him tell her that.

But from the panicked look in her eyes and the way she was leaning back, his feelings were the last things she wanted to hear.

Her hand came up and rested on his arm. She smiled up at him, and from the look in her eyes, he was not going to like what she had to say.

"I love you like a friend. That's all." She paused as her gaze roamed over his face.

Was he that obvious? Could she see that her words were killing him? His heart was breaking in a way that he doubted could ever heal.

He'd broken up with so many girls in his past, but this was different. Getting rejected by the one woman who knew so much about him was worse.

"Tiffany, I—"

"Please, Jonathan, don't do this." Her voice had dropped to a whisper as she stared up at him, a pleading look in her eyes.

"Do what?" What did she think he was going to do? And why was wanting to love her bad? Was it him?

She swallowed. "Whatever it is you are going to do, please don't. I can't...I can't lose you as a friend. You mean too much to me."

It felt as if she'd just slapped him in the face. Why was she fighting this? All he wanted to do was to love her and have her love him back. Was that so wrong?

But she looked so small and broken, standing in front of him with a desperate look in her eyes, that he couldn't just push past her concerns and confess. That wasn't love, and he didn't want to hurt her. It was his job to protect her—even if it meant protecting her from him.

He sighed and then smiled as he reached down and pulled her into a hug. "I'm sorry," he said with his lips muffled by her hair. The smell of her coconut shampoo surrounded him. It caused the hole in his heart to ache.

As much as he wanted her, she would never be his, and he needed to accept that.

Tiffany let out a soft sob as she wrapped her arms around him and buried her face into his shirt. They stood there, in the middle of the dance floor, holding each other.

It wasn't until the song ended and a lighter, pop song started blaring from the speakers that they pulled apart.

Jonathan smiled down at her, even though his soul ached to pull her back. To never let her go.

Tiffany looked relieved as she wiped her eyes. Then she smiled up at him. "I should probably go find Cody," she said.

Jonathan nodded. "I'll come with you."

Her eyebrows rose. "Really? Why? Don't you have a leggy blonde to get back to?"

Jonathan shrugged. "Shelby? I don't know where she went off to. I think I annoyed her." Truth was, he had ditched her. He didn't want to string her along if there wasn't anything that could happen between them. He doubted anyone would entice him anymore. Not when his heart belonged to the one woman who didn't want him.

Tiffany patted his arm. "Well, I'm sure we'll find someone for you." She waved her hand around the crowded bar. "There's lots of eligible women here. I'm sure one of them will pass the Jonathan test."

Jonathan just nodded. He wasn't comfortable with pretending to let Tiffany set him up anymore. If anything, he just wanted her to drop it.

"There you are," Cody's voice pulled Jonathan's attention over.

It took all his strength not to reach out and punch Cody in his smug face. And then he felt bad. Cody didn't know what was going on. To him, Tiffany was a girl that he was interested in. Someone who wasn't tied to anyone else.

Why should that make him mad?

"Can we go get a drink?" Tiffany asked as she turned and smiled up at him.

Cody nodded. "Of course. Anything for you."

Tiffany turned and studied Jonathan as Cody led her over

to the bar. Jonathan couldn't help but hold her gaze as she walked past him.

He wanted to reach out. To tell her not to go. She should stay with him...he loved her. But she just smiled and shifted her attention over to Cody, who was telling her about the different types of drinks he liked.

Now alone, Jonathan contemplated either walking over to join them or leaving. If Tiffany wanted someone here so she could save face with her family, Cody would fill that void just fine. Besides, it wasn't like he knew anyone else here. What would it matter if he left?

Turning, he kept his head down as he made his way off the dance floor and ran right into someone. Startled, he glanced up to see Beatrice standing there with a teasing look on her face.

"Hey," she said, reaching out to rest her hand on his arm. "Are you okay?"

Clearing his throat, Jonathan nodded. "Yeah, of course. Why?"

She studied him and then shrugged. "Nothing." Then she smiled. "How's your evening going?"

It was almost nice to have someone other than Tiffany to talk to. It was more relaxed than trying to wade through the pain associated with his best friend.

"Well..." He shrugged as he winked down at her. Flirting with someone when it meant nothing was actually calming. There was no stress that went along with it.

Beatrice dropped her jaw in an exaggerated movement. "Well, we just might have to remedy that. Come on." She slid her hand down his arm and into his hand. Then she tugged, pulling him along after her.

Chuckling, Jonathan followed as she led him over to the bar—on the other side of Tiffany and Cody.

Jonathan couldn't help but let his gaze flick over to Tiffany, who was staring at him, aghast. When their eyes met, Jonathan mustered the courage to wave at her and then shoot her a thumbs-up.

Tiffany closed her lips and smiled, returning the gesture. Then she moved her attention over to Cody, who looked as if he were waiting for an answer. Tiffany laughed —a bit too loud—and then leaned in to rest her hand on Cody's arm.

Standing there and staring at them wasn't going to fix the hole in his heart, so Jonathan turned his attention over to Beatrice. She had picked up the drink that the bartender had just set down and turned to hand him one.

Jonathan took it and smiled down at her.

He needed to move on from Tiffany. Especially since it seemed like he was the only one whose feelings had changed. If he was going to even attempt to maintain his friendship with the woman who'd rejected him, he needed to find someone else and fast.

And Beatrice was here, staring at him with a wide smile.

She'd have to do.

Jonathan spent the evening trying to carry a conversation with Beatrice while ignoring the fact that Cody was standing too close to Tiffany or the way his fingers were playing with her hair.

There were a few times that he had to stifle the desire to walk over there and pull Cody off of Tiffany when he leaned in and almost kissed her.

Thankfully, Tiffany didn't notice and turned her head just in time, narrowly missing Cody's lips.

By the time he got back to his hotel room, Jonathan was

exhausted. He bid a disappointed Beatrice good night and headed over to the elevator, where he pressed the up button.

Thankfully, no one tried to board with him as the doors slid shut.

Now alone, he let out a sigh as he leaned against one of the elevator walls. He stared at his hands as he tried to sort through all the emotions coursing through him.

What was he going to do? How was he going to survive the rest of this trip? He hated having a front seat to Tiffany's blossoming new romance.

Ugh.

He fisted his hands and exited the elevator. He swiped his room key and pushed into the room.

The door shut behind him with a resounding thud.

Exhaustion getting the better of him, he made his way over to the bed and flopped down face-first. He lay there until the sound of a keycard trying to open the door drew his attention.

He heard Tiffany's exasperated sigh and two muffled voices.

He shook his head as he pushed off the bed and headed over to the door. He could do this. He could be strong. If he didn't want to lose Tiffany as a friend, he needed to buck up and get over the feelings that were swarming his mind.

He pushed down hard on the door handle and swung the door open to find a very startled Tiffany. Her eyes were wide and her lips parted in an "o."

"Hey," he said, holding the door open with his arm.

"Hey…" She glanced behind him and into the room. "I, um, I didn't expect you back so early."

His gaze flicked over to Cody, who was leaning against the wall with an amused look on his face.

"Yeah, I was tired. Beatrice was tired. We decided to call it a night."

Tiffany furrowed her brow. "Oh. I saw Beatrice in the lobby bar. So maybe she wasn't as tired?"

Jonathan shrugged. "Well, I was beat."

Tiffany nodded as she fiddled with the keycard in her hand. "Well, Cody was just dropping me off."

"Oh." An awkward feeling fell around them, so Jonathan flipped the lock to the door and moved back into the room. "I'll just leave this so you can get back in."

Tiffany's cheeks flushed and she looked like she was going to say something, but Jonathan wasn't sure he wanted to hear it. The last thing he needed was for her to define her new relationship with Cody. He wasn't sure he could take another emotional hit like that.

"I'll be in here, not listening," he said as the door closed on them.

Frustration brewed in his stomach as he made his way over to the bed and sat down. After a few seconds, he let out a growl and went in search of the remote. There was no reason that saying goodbye should take this long, which meant only one thing—and that one thing was the last thing he wanted to be thinking about.

He clicked the power button and began to scroll through the channels. He landed on the news and turned the volume up. He really wasn't listening to what was being said, he just needed a distraction.

A few minutes later, Tiffany slipped into the room, letting the door close behind her. Jonathan studied her expression from the corner of his eye. Did she look happy? Did she really like that guy?

He cleared his throat as he focused his attention back to the TV.

Tiffany stepped closer to the bed. Not sure what she was doing, he glanced over at her and smiled. "Have a fun time?" he asked.

Tiffany leaned in. "What?"

Realizing that she couldn't hear him over the TV, he clicked the volume down to a manageable decibel.

"Did you have a fun time?"

Tiffany sat down on the corner of the bed and studied him. "Yeah. Cody is nice."

Jonathan swallowed hard as he forced a smile. "Well, that's good. Cody seems like an alright guy." He shrugged like he didn't care. Anything to save face with Tiffany.

"He is."

Jonathan's cheeks hurt from how hard he was smiling. Turns out a fake smile is a lot harder to manage then a real one. Plus, what was up with their conversation? Was this really what they'd come to? Awkward one-liners?

Ugh.

Their relationship was over before it ever began.

Frustrated with how he was feeling, Jonathan pushed off the bed and headed over to the fridge to pull out a bottle of water. Once it was half gone, he twisted the lid back on and set it on the dresser next to the TV.

He turned around to see Tiffany staring off into the distance. She was studying the wall and looked as if she had a lot on her mind.

Normally he'd ask her what was wrong, but he wasn't sure if that was overstepping anymore. After she'd rejected him earlier at the bar, he wasn't sure he could handle her doing that again. He sighed and rolled his shoulders as he moved over to one of the dresser drawers and pulled it open. Maybe they had something to read in one of them.

Anything to make him look distracted.

"Looking for something?" Tiffany asked.

Jonathan slammed one of the drawers—probably a bit too hard. Turning, he shrugged. "A book. Something."

She studied him for a moment before she exhaled and flopped back on the bed.

"What's happening to us?" she whispered, almost as if she hadn't meant to say it out loud.

Jonathan's heart began to race as he stepped forward. Had he heard her right? What did that mean?

"What?" he asked.

Tiffany pinched her lips together as she stared up at the ceiling. So she *had* been trying to keep it a secret.

"Jonathan, let it go," she said as she reached her hands up to her face and began massaging her temples.

"Let what go?" For some inane reason, he thought it was wise to walk over to her. Like facing her was the best way to get her to tell the truth.

She closed her eyes. "Whatever you think is going on."

He needed her to look him in the eyes. He needed her to tell him that it was hopeless. There was no way he was going to be able to move on if she didn't know how he felt.

"Why are you doing this?" he asked, his voice coming out rough.

Tiffany stilled, her eyes closed. Then she slowly opened them. "Jonathan, I can't—"

"Can't or won't?"

She glanced over at him and then slowly sat up. She stood, moving toward the window and peering out. "I like Cody. I'm sorry."

No. There was no way he could believe that. She'd just met the guy. "Typical Tiffany," he said as he walked over to the TV and turned it off.

She whipped around, a fiery look in her eyes. "'Excuse me?"

Jonathan met her frustration with the same amount of intensity. He wasn't going to let her off the hook. She was running away and she knew it. She always ran from what was real. "You're a coward."

Her eyebrows rose as her lips parted. "I'm a what?"

Jonathan stood his ground. He was her best friend. It was his job to call her on her crap. "You're being a coward. You're afraid of love."

She stepped forward, her hand raised as if she were trying to stop the words lingering in the air. "I am not a coward. And what about you? Running from any meaningful relationship."

He studied her. "What?"

She held up her fingers and pointed them in his direction. "When was the last time you had a relationship that lasted longer than a Tic Tac?"

Jonathan shook his head. "I'm not the one on trial here. I'm not the one fighting my feelings."

Her expression softened as she studied him. "What does that mean?" she whispered as she dropped her hand.

"I think you know," he said, stepping forward, the desire to touch her overpowering him. He needed her to know how he felt even if she was never going to let him say it.

"Jonathan," she breathed as he approached her. She didn't move to back away, which he took as a good sign.

Throwing caution to the wind, he wrapped his arms around her waist and pulled her against him. Every part of him needed to touch her. To feel her close.

"Tiffany," he whispered, dipping down to press his lips to hers.

The room around him stilled as she tensed. Worried he'd done something wrong, he moved to pull away. But Tiffany wouldn't let him. Instead, she raised her hands up to his neck and entwined her fingers in his hair, crushing his mouth to hers.

Jonathan let out a growl as he reached down and pulled her legs up around his waist. He held her steady as his mouth explored hers.

Every part of him needed her to know that she was the one. He needed this kiss to say everything that he hadn't been able to say. That he was in love with her.

He made his way over to the bed and sat her down gently. He focused on her lips as she parted them and allowed him in.

This was so much more than a kiss. She was finally admitting that there was something more than friendship between the two of them. This kiss meant they just might have a chance at what he so desperately wanted.

For her to love him back.

He pulled back and met her gaze, studying every part of her face. She was pure perfection. How had he never seen that before.

Her hands were warm as they explored his chest, arms, and back.

He dropped down onto his elbows so he could brush her hair from her face. Then he leaned in and pressed his lips gently to her forehead, temple, and then cheek.

She let out a soft sigh, and it stirred a hunger inside of him. He wanted Tiffany. All of her.

He moved to press his lips to hers again, but this time, she pushed against his chest. Confused, he pulled back to study her.

Instead of the hazy-eyed girl that had been kissing him before, she was wide-eyed and panicked. Like she'd just made the biggest mistake of her life.

"I—I need to go to the bathroom," she said.

Worried he'd done something wrong, he nodded and stood, allowing her to slip past him. She didn't look back as she hurried into the bathroom and shut the door.

Now alone, Jonathan sat down on the bed. Thoughts swirled around in his mind. Part of him was deliriously happy. He was in love with his best friend.

The other part of him worried that there was no way she felt the same.

CHAPTER FOURTEEN

Oh crap. Oh crap, oh crap, oh *crap*.

What had she just done?

Tiffany stood on the other side of the bathroom door, pressing her hand to her stomach. Everything was in knots—good and bad.

But her head was screaming at her.

This was not what she'd decided on. It was the exact opposite. She was supposed to stay away from Jonathan, not assault his lips.

Groaning out of frustration, she made her way over to the toilet and sat on the lid. She dropped her head into her hands and closed her eyes.

She could still see Jonathan staring down at her with so much feeling in his gaze that it took her breath away. He cared about her. A lot. And she'd allowed him to believe that was an okay thing to do.

Like she wasn't going to break his heart, even though she knew she was going to do.

Why was she so dumb? She shouldn't have allowed any of this to happen.

Never mind the fact that she would have to go back out there and tell Jonathan that it had been a huge mistake, she was now going to have to live with the fact that she'd broken his heart. He'd handed it to her, and she'd taken it and then stomped all over it.

She was the worst friend in existence.

Tears welled up in her eyes, and she tipped her face up to squelch them. She didn't deserve to feel like this. She'd been the one to let her guard down and let Jonathan get sucked into her messed-up world. The world where she disappointed every guy she'd ever been with.

Once Jonathan realized how ridiculous she was, he would want to leave. He'd walk out the door and abandon her. Just like her mom did. Just like every man in her life did.

She was born to be alone. She should accept that before she hurt anyone else.

She needed to stop feeling sorry for herself and be the bigger person. Face Jonathan like he deserved. She needed to tell him that the kiss was a huge mistake. That she knew he would be upset, but she hoped he'd forgive her and they could move forward…as friends.

Just as she thought the last few words, her chest squeezed. That wasn't what she wanted. Not at all.

She wanted to be more than friends. She wanted him. All of him. She'd been friends with him for so long, and she knew what that was like.

But now? She wanted to be his. She wanted to wake up next to him and fall asleep at night with him by her side.

She wanted to have his children.

Shaking her head, she scolded herself. Was she an idiot? What was wrong with her?

Jonathan deserved so much better than her. He deserved a woman. A perfect woman. And she was far from that.

She wrapped her arms around her chest and stared over

at the sink. She knew what lay on the other side of the wall, and she wasn't sure if she could handle disappointing him. It was breaking her heart just thinking about it.

"He deserves better," she whispered to herself. He deserved so much better.

She swallowed as she stood and turned on the shower. She needed some time away from him if she was going to survive. After throwing her hair up into a bun, she slipped under the hot water, allowing it to beat against her tense muscles.

She closed her eyes as she played back the kiss in her mind.

It was mind blowing. Everything she thought a kiss should be. Every other kiss she'd experienced paled in comparison to his.

The way he made her feel shocked her. It made her feel vulnerable and scared, something she hadn't allowed herself to feel, and yet, the fact that it was Jonathan soothed her. She trusted him.

Frustrated with the thoughts pounding against her skull, she flipped off the water and grabbed a towel. She needed to get out of here. She needed distance from him.

After slipping on her clothes, she pulled her hair down and took a deep breath. She just needed to leave the room before he noticed.

Which was probably not likely, but she could do it.

She rested her hand on the doorknob and counted down. She turned the handle and kept her gaze on the floor as she located her shoes.

"Tiffany?" Jonathan's low and confused voice caused her to shiver.

She was hurting him, she could tell. But it was better for her to leave now before she hurt him more. Just like ripping off a Band-Aid.

"I have to go," she whispered, emotions choking her throat.

"But..." His hand reached out and wrapped around her arm.

Tiffany fought the tears that were threatening to spill. If Jonathan saw them, then he'd know they were for him and he'd never let her go. Hadn't he always said it was his job to protect her? Call her crazy, but she was pretty sure he would categorize this as something she needed saving from.

"I have to go," She repeated as she grabbed her purse and pushed it up onto her shoulder. She turned and hurried over to the door, where she reached out to grab the handle.

"Hang on," he said. The panic in his voice caused her to stop.

She hated what she was doing to him. He was her friend. He deserved to have her hear him out.

"What?" she asked, braving heartbreak as she glanced up at him.

Thankfully, he wasn't looking at her. Instead, he was digging around in his wallet. He emerged with a keycard. When his gaze met hers, her heart nearly stopped.

He was in pain. So much pain. She was the reason he was hurting. She'd spent so much time trying to stop this exact thing, but she'd ended up doing it anyways.

Hurting the people she loved.

"Here. In case you want to come back." He held up the keycard in front of her.

Tiffany parted her lips as she raised her hand and wrapped her fingers around the card. There was so much she wanted to say but couldn't. He'd think he had a chance if she spoke.

So she just nodded, slipped the card from his hand, and grabbed the door handle.

It wasn't until she was on the other side of the door that

she allowed herself to breathe again. But it wasn't a smooth inhalation. It was staggered and rough. It matched how she felt inside perfectly.

Closing her eyes, she calmed her nerves enough to walk down the hall. She didn't want people to see her and assume there was a crazy person in the hotel. That was the last thing she needed.

Once she was sure she at least appeared calm, she pushed off the wall and made her way down to the elevator. She wasn't really sure where she was going, she just knew that she couldn't stay here.

She boarded the elevator and took it down to the lobby. Once the doors opened on the foyer, she took in a deep breath. She could do this. It was the right thing.

Even though doubt tugged at her mind, she shook it off and stepped out onto the marble floor. She glanced around to find some of the wedding party milling around in the bar to the left.

If she were honest with herself, she really didn't want to go socialize with her family. She just wanted to be alone.

But as she rounded the corner, a very loud squeal drew her attention over to Stacy, who rushed over to her and wrapped her into a hug.

"Hey, coz!" she exclaimed rather loudly in Tiffany's ear.

She winced and hugged her cousin back. "Hey, Stacy."

Stacy giggled as she pulled back. "I'm getting married tomorrow," she whispered. Her eyes were wide, and for a moment, Tiffany saw some worry behind her cousin's normally cheery gaze.

Worried that Stacy was having doubts, she pulled back and wrapped her arm around her cousin's shoulders.

"What's going on?" she asked.

Stacy sniffled as she shrugged. "It's just a lot, you know. The commitment. What if…what if he gets bored with me?

What will happen once I have kids and my boobs are hanging on the floor?" She started to wail, drawing the attention of people passing by.

Tiffany shushed her cousin as she led Stacy over to the elevator. "Let's get you upstairs and get you in your pajamas. I'm sure you're just overwhelmed."

Stacy mumbled something about needing her girls and shoved her phone into Tiffany's hand as the elevator doors shut and the car began to rise.

Tiffany found the group text she'd been on and messaged everyone to meet up in Stacy's room for some girl time Everyone responded with a thumbs-up, and just as they neared Stacy's suite, Tiffany found them all standing outside. Each had some sort of beauty item in their hands.

Stacy squealed as she reached out and engulfed them all in a big hug. Chatter rose up around them as Tiffany took the keycard from Stacy and swiped the door.

They spilled into the room. Tiffany lingered in the hallway as she glanced around. Where was Beatrice?

When she got into Stacy's room, she glanced over at Heather, who was laughing as she opened the minibar.

"Really, Heather? Do you have a love of blinding headaches?" Tiffany said as she nodded toward the alcohol.

Heather shrugged. "I'll be fine."

Tiffany shook her head. One of the reasons she watched what she drank was because she hated how out of control she felt. Plus, she'd done some pretty stupid things in her past when she was wasted, and she'd learned the hard way that it was the last thing she needed.

Heather took a mini bottle and slipped into the bathroom, where she declared that she was starting the bath so they could do pedicures.

Tiffany followed her inside and sat down on the toilet lid. She wanted to ask where Beatrice was without sounding desperate. After rubbing her palms on her thighs a few times, she took a deep breath.

"Hey, Heather?"

Heather turned and nodded at her. "What's up?"

"Where's Beatrice?"

Heather studied her. Then she shrugged as she dipped her fingers into the water. "I think she was off to check on Jonathan or something."

Tiffany's stomach lurched. Beatrice went to check on Jonathan? What did that mean?

And then she felt stupid. She knew what that meant. She knew exactly what Beatrice was trying to do. It was something she wouldn't have thought twice about doing before.

She must have looked awful, because Heather's eyebrows rose as she looked at Tiffany. "What's with you? I thought you two broke up."

Tiffany let out her breath as she sat down on the floor and wrapped her arms around her knees, hugging them to her chest. "Can I tell you a secret?"

Heather's eyes widened as she nodded. "Always."

Tiffany swallowed as she closed her eyes for a moment. "Jonathan was never my boyfriend. He's been my best friend since we were kids." Her voice drifted off as her emotions rose up in her chest. Everything about this weekend felt as if it were crushing her. Like if she took a moment to think about where her relationship was with Jonathan, she might break.

When Heather didn't say anything, Tiffany glanced over at her.

"Why lie?" Heather asked, leaning over to flip off the water.

Tiffany buried her face in her hands. "I didn't want to prove to everyone that, yet again, I suck at relationships. The boyfriend I was going to bring dumped me last week. Jonathan offered to come as my date so I could save face."

Heather nodded. "And you fell in love with him."

Tiffany choked on her tongue as she turned to study her friend. "What?"

Heather snorted. "Oh, come on, Tiffany, it's so obvious. You're always looking at him. You blush when he touches you. You looked like you were about to claw Beatrice's face off when I told you she's off visiting him." Heather clicked her tongue. "It's pretty obvious you have feelings for him."

Tiffany cradled her head in her hands. As much as she hated that Heather had pegged the situation perfectly, she wasn't sure it was good for her to hear.

It was easy enough to ignore her feelings when she didn't acknowledge them. But now they were staring her in the face, forcing her to confront them. And she didn't like it.

"Heather, I can't. What if I fail? What if I lose him for good?" Tiffany glanced over at Heather, pleading for the answer to her situation.

Heather took in a deep breath and shrugged. "It's up to you. I mean, if you love him, take the chance. But if you don't think that's something you can do, then you need to let him go." She reached over and ran her fingers through the water. "It's not fair to string him along."

Tiffany twisted until she was kneeling by the tub and dipped her fingers into the water. It felt good. In a way, it sort of shocked her system into remembering that she was alive.

"And if I lose him?" She glanced over at Heather.

Heather gave her a soft smile. "From what I've seen when he looks at you, he's not going anywhere. I doubt you could fight him off with a stick. That boy loves you. And I'm sure your friendship means more to him than anything."

Tiffany's heart began to pound at Heather's words.

Jonathan loved her. And if she loved him back, she needed to let him go. He deserved someone better than her. Someone much better.

Heather sighed. "I know that look," she said, leaning over to bump Tiffany's shoulder with her own.

Tiffany studied her. "What?"

"You're going to run."

Tiffany pulled her fingers from the water and flicked the excess water from her fingers before reaching over to grab a towel. "You said if I loved him, I'd let him go."

Heather snorted. "Of course that would be the only thing you heard."

Confused, Tiffany sat down on the toilet seat. "But you said—"

"Out of everything I said, that was what you fixated on? Letting him go? Walking away?"

"But—"

"Tiffany, you have to start believing that you are worthy of love. You need to forget whatever happened in the past and focus on the present. What's staring you in the face." Heather's expression softened. "Because what you have with him is about as real as you're ever going to get."

Tiffany studied her cousin. She wanted to admit that Heather was right. But she couldn't. Not when things were so confusing and muddled in her mind.

"I know," she whispered, but before she could say anything more, two giggling bridesmaids burst into the room with flutes of champagne.

"We're here for our pedicures," they said in unison as they kicked off their flip-flops and stumbled over to the tub.

Taking this as her cue to leave, Tiffany waved to Heather and slipped out of the bathroom.

She spent the rest of the night curled up on the armchair in Stacy's room. She really wasn't in the mood to party.

Besides, someone had to keep the other girls from calling up ex-boyfriends or ordering a stripper.

At two in the morning, there was a knock on the door. Tiffany sidestepped a few of the girls who had passed out on the floor and made her way over. She opened the door to reveal Beatrice.

She looked happy. And it made Tiffany sick to her stomach.

"Hey," Tiffany said as she leaned on the door.

Beatrice smiled at her and then peeked over Tiffany's shoulder. "Sorry. I was…busy. Are they still up?"

Tiffany shook her head. Even if they were, she would have lied to Beatrice. There was no way she wanted to sit in the same room as her. Not when Beatrice had just spent the evening with Jonathan—doing who knows what.

No. Right now, she needed Beatrice to leave so she could keep her sanity.

"Oh. Then I'll probably head to bed," Beatrice said as she folded her arms over her chest.

"Sounds good," Tiffany said as she began to shut the door.

"Hey, Tiff?"

Tiffany hesitated and then turned. "Yeah?"

"You should talk to Jonathan. He's confused and worried he lost you as a friend."

Tiffany winced. He'd talked to Beatrice about her? What was she supposed to say to that? Mustering her strength, Tiffany nodded. "Okay. I will."

Beatrice gave her a soft smile and then turned and headed down the hallway.

Tiffany shut the door and collapsed against it. She pinched her lips as tears welled up in her eyes.

How could things have gotten so bad so fast?

CHAPTER FIFTEEN

The next morning, Jonathan sat on the bed with one leg brought up and his ankle was resting on his knee. He was showered and getting dressed for the wedding he'd been roped into being in.

At the time, it had felt great. Helping out Tiffany's cousin was, in a way, helping out Tiffany. But now she was mad at him. She hadn't even come back to the room last night.

He'd really screwed up when he'd kissed her.

His lips burned from the memory of her lips pressed to his. That was the part that killed him. She'd kissed him back. He was sure he hadn't made that up. Tiffany cared about him the same way he cared about her. He could feel it in his bones.

But she was running, and there didn't seem to be anything he could do to stop her.

Sighing, he slipped on his sock and then moved to put on the other one. Then he leaned over to grab his shoes.

His phone rang next to him. Resting the shoes on the bed, he grabbed it to see that it was James, his younger brother.

A smile played on his lips as he hit the talk button.

"Hey, loser," he said with all the affection he could muster.

"Nice." James's deep voice caused him to chuckle.

"What's up?" he asked as he untied his shoes and slipped his feet into them.

"Not much. Just calling to see how things are there. Mom wanted me to check in with you guys, so that's what I'm doing."

Jonathan shrugged. Even though he was going through something right now, the last thing he wanted to do was tell James. At least, not until he'd worked through whatever was going on. "I'm at a wedding with Tiffany," he said, hoping he sounded more relaxed than he felt.

"Yeah? How's that going?"

Jonathan closed his eyes as he shook his head. "Well, you know. Beating the single ladies off with a stick."

James chuckled. "Yep. Sounds about right. Did you hear about Josh and Beth? Crazy, huh?"

Jonathan chuckled. "Not if you were here. Josh is whipped." His heart squeezed at the thought of his brother finally finding the girl of his dreams. At least she wanted him. Tiffany was more than ready to run away than to face what they could have.

"Mom's ecstatic. Josh said she's already saving a date."

"Sounds like Mom."

"I told him if he does get married, I'll make sure to come out for it. Mom must have heard. So, be prepared to be pressured."

Jonathan nodded. "Will do, man. But, hey, I'm part of the wedding party and I need to finish getting ready. Can I call you later?"

"Yep."

"Perfect. I'll talk to you then."

"Bye."

Jonathan said goodbye and then hung up the phone. He

set it next to him and let out his breath and the stress that was building up inside of him. He loved the fact that he'd been able to talk with his brother, but it'd only reminded him of how alone he felt and how badly he wanted to connect with a certain someone.

And that someone was the one person who seemed as if she wanted nothing to do with him.

The sound of a keycard at the door drew his attention over. His head raced as he stared at the door, wondering if it was Tiffany on the other side.

When the door opened, and Tiffany walked through, he wanted to celebrate and crawl under the bed at the same time. He studied her face, wondering if she was going to give anything away. Was she still mad at him?

"Hey," he said, standing to greet her. He moved toward her, but from the panicked look on her face, he pulled back. He dipped down so that he could study her. "Everything okay?"

Tiffany nodded. "Yes. I spent the night in Stacy's room. Sort of a last-minute hurrah before today." She pressed on her hair that was styled in an up-do. "And then we went and got our hair done." She met his gaze and gave him a sheepish smile. "I hope I didn't worry you."

He held her gaze, hoping she could see that he wasn't angry. Sad, yes. But he couldn't be mad at her. He loved her too much. And if she needed him to back off, he would. "No, not worried."

She pinched her lips together and then ducked her head to make her way over to the mirror. She started pulling out her makeup and setting it on the counter.

He wasn't willing to let that be the end of their conversation. He was going to talk to her even if she didn't want him to. He was going to stay her friend. He wouldn't just let her run away.

"So, Stacy's, huh? Anything crazy happen last night?"

Tiffany paused with a makeup brush in her hand. She lifted her gaze up until it met Jonathan's in the mirror. She looked at him for a moment and then shrugged. "Not really. Pedicures and alcohol. Those ladies can drink me under the table." A soft smile played on the edges of her lips as she got a far-off look in her eyes.

"I can see it."

She glanced back at him and nodded. "Beatrice came a bit late, though."

At the mention of Beatrice, Jonathan shifted his weight. He knew that it probably hadn't been the smartest decision, letting her into his room last night. But he needed to talk to someone about Tiffany. A family member felt like a safe bet.

"She was here," he said. There was no way he wanted her to think that anything had happened between them. He didn't like Beatrice like that, and he would never do that to Tiffany. "We just talked. That was it."

Tiffany's forehead furrowed. "I know. She told me." She smiled over at him. It felt forced and insincere. "It's okay. You're single. You can date who you want to."

Jonathan's ears rang at her words. That was not what he was expecting her to say. "I—"

"We got carried away last night, that's all. Probably a bit too much drinking was involved in the making of those events." She smiled again, this time showing more teeth. "I don't hold you accountable for your actions, just as I'm sure you don't hold me to mine."

Wow. Talk about a sucker punch to the gut. Before, it had been easy to believe that she was just hurting. But a complete denial of last night was not what he'd expected. How could she be so cavalier about the whole situation?

He'd been there last night. He'd felt her pressed against him. She'd kissed him back—she'd wanted him as badly as he wanted her. Tiffany was a good actress, but she wasn't that good.

He glanced up to see her focused on her makeup. He wanted to say something back. He wanted to correct her, to get her to say what he knew was in her heart. But he doubted she would.

So he pushed off the wall and walked across the room to grab his suit coat.

How could she act this relaxed? He knew she felt something too.

After shoving his arms through and pulling the jacket up onto his shoulders, he made his way over to the window and stared down at the pool below. The water glistened in the morning sun, making him want to jump in just to see the water interrupted.

He needed to get out of this room. Out of the awkwardness that surrounded the two of them.

The sound of the bathroom door softly shutting caused him to glance over his shoulder. Tiffany wasn't in the room.

Not wanting to stand by the window anymore, Jonathan turned and made his way over to the bed, where he sat down. He hung his head as he took a few deep breaths.

This was not the way he should be approaching this. If she needed space, he should give it to her. If he still wanted her friendship, then he needed to play by her rules no matter how much it hurt.

A few minutes later, she emerged, dressed in a gold satin dress. She looked...beautiful.

Jonathan itched to take her into his arms and tell her how he felt, despite the consequences, and lay everything out on the line.

Her gaze met his as she made her way over to her suitcase and grabbed her shoes. Jonathan cleared his throat as he gave her a quick smile, hoping to mask the pain he felt.

"You look amazing," he said in his normal, flirty voice.

Tiffany stopped and turned her gaze up to him. "Thanks," she said. Her eyebrows were raised as she studied him, and then she turned back to digging through her clothes.

"I mean that in a friend type of way," he said, holding up his hands.

She glanced over at him. "Okay."

Worried that he was stepping over the line, he chuckled. But instead of it coming out relaxed, it sounded as forced as it felt. "I've moved on from last night. You're right. It was a drunken mistake." He held up his left hand. "I promise never to bring it up or try that again." He morphed his expression into one that he hoped came across as disgusted.

Tiffany's expression stilled as she met his gaze. She held it for a moment, and Jonathan almost passed out from the confusion he felt. What was she thinking about? Had he said something wrong? He swore that being just friends was what she'd wanted. But now? He didn't know.

And he hated that he felt so confused.

Thankfully, she gave him a soft smile and nodded. "Sounds good." She approached him with her hand extended. "Friends?"

He stared at her hand and then grabbed it, forcing down all the feelings that rose up inside of him from her touch. He couldn't feel that way for her, and the sooner he fought it off, the better.

He wanted Tiffany in his life no matter what.

"Friends," he said. He shook her hand a few more times and then smiled over at her. "Luke needs his Leia."

Tiffany nodded, the sides of her lips tipping up into a smile. "Agreed."

They stood there for a few seconds. Jonathan felt the tension he'd been feeling this whole trip slowly fade. He was standing next to his best friend. The one girl that had stayed in his life. She was the constant lighthouse that he always came back to.

She was his everything. And he couldn't lose that.

He nodded toward the door. "Shall we? Stacy and Rob need to get married."

Tiffany let out a deep sigh and nodded. "Yeah they do. She's was all sorts of crazy last night. I had to talk her off a cliff."

Jonathan chuckled as he followed Tiffany out into the hallway.

"You're a good cousin. That was nice of you to take care of her."

Tiffany nodded as she adjusted the skirt of her dress. "Well, it's what I would want on my wedding day. My family having my back. Even though certain members of it have sucked."

Jonathan glanced over at her. He knew what she was talking about. Her dad. The man who left so many years ago and was never heard from again save the yearly Christmas card he sent with a photo of his new family tucked inside of it.

The one guy who'd disappointed Tiffany over and over again.

They walked to the elevator in silence, and Jonathan pressed the down button. Once the doors opened, Jonathan stepped inside, followed by Tiffany.

The door closed and soft orchestra music filled the silence. Jonathan peeked over at Tiffany, wondering what she was thinking. Was she thinking about him? Was it wrong that he hoped she was?

"So I got a call from James," he said, shoving his hands into his pants pockets.

Tiffany glanced over at him. "Really? What's he up to?"

Jonathan shrugged. "Apparently Mom's been calling all of

us to tell us about Josh and Beth's relationship. I have a feeling she's hoping it inspires us to follow suit."

Tiffany laughed. It was melodious and familiar. She tipped her head back, exposing the feminine curves to her neck. Her skin looked smooth and touchable.

Blinking a few times helped him clear his mind. That was not what he was supposed to be thinking about. She was his friend. That was it.

"Your mom," Tiffany said as her laughter died down. She reached up to dab at her eyes. "She's my favorite."

Jonathan nodded. "She's great. She definitely means well."

Tiffany glanced over at him, her smile open and unabashed. "She does. You're lucky."

"Yeah. I am."

The elevator's doors slid open, exposing the members of the wedding party who were lingering in the foyer. Jonathan followed Tiffany out. He tried not to stare when Cody walked up to Tiffany and pulled her into a hug. He also tried hard not to stare when Tiffany pulled away and leaned in to talk to him. What was she saying?

Cody's smile widened as he nodded. Then he leaned in, gave her a hug, and waved toward the pool where he'd be serving drinks later. He made some motion with his hands like he was typing numbers into a phone, but Tiffany just shrugged and reached out to brush her fingers against his arm.

Jonathan had never felt so frustrated. He wanted to know what was going on, but he couldn't see Tiffany's face or hear what was being said. He wanted to hope that she was breaking things off, but that felt like a fool's errand.

"Hey," Beatrice's soft voice startled him. She was peering up at him with a smile on her lips. Her hair was pulled up in the same way Tiffany's was, and she was wearing the same dress.

"Hey," he said, grateful for the distraction. Before he knew what he was doing, he reached out and pulled her into a hug.

It had felt right in theory, but holding her against him didn't have the same effect on his soul as holding Tiffany. Beatrice was just a stand-in for the person he really wanted.

Feeling like a fool, he pulled back and scrubbed his face. He couldn't lead Beatrice on. It wasn't fair to her. He pulled back, but kept his hand resting on her arm. When she glanced up at him, he cursed himself. He should have never lead her on. That was wrong of him.

"Hey, Beatrice," he said, dipping down to meet her gaze.

Beatrice studied him. "Yeah?"

"I hope…I hope I haven't led you on or anything."

A strained smile spread across her lips. "What? I—"

"It's just that I have feelings for someone else, and it wouldn't be fair to you to not tell you." He dropped his hand as he gave her a soft smile.

She studied him for a moment and then sighed. "I understand." She turned to focus on the wedding coordinator, who was waving them down. She took a step forward and then paused. "She's lucky, even if she doesn't know that." Beatrice met his gaze and then glanced over to where Tiffany stood.

Jonathan followed her eyes to find that Cody had left and Tiffany was standing there, alone, just staring at them. As his gaze met hers, she dropped her eyes to study the floor.

Jonathan tried to ignore the fact that his heart picked up speed from her attention. Instead, he glanced back down at Beatrice and nodded. "Thanks."

She smiled. "If she rejects you for good, I'm always here." She winked as she followed the other bridesmaids, including Tiffany, to stand in front of the bride.

Jonathan followed the groomsmen and got in line. He glanced over to see that Tiffany had been paired up with him. She met his gaze and gave him an uneasy smile.

All Jonathan could do was shrug. It wasn't ideal, but he couldn't imagine walking down the aisle with anyone else. He needed to figure out how to fix their relationship even if the outcome wasn't everything he wanted.

All he knew was that Tiffany was in his life for the long haul, no matter what.

He wasn't going anywhere.

CHAPTER SIXTEEN

Tiffany kept her gaze down on her flowers as the line moved. In two seconds, she was going to have to link arms with Jonathan and walk down the aisle with him.

Her stomach was in knots.

She took in a deep breath and let it out slowly. She could do this.

She linked arms with him, and a shiver raced up her arm. Her heart pounded from his touch, making her feel light-headed and dizzy.

And like an idiot. Being just friends was never going to work if she kept having a reaction to him every time they touched. Every time they talked.

This was not off to a good start.

They started down the aisle, walking in sync with each other. Even though her head was telling her to run, her heart was telling her this was where she belonged. With Jonathan.

"Tiffany, I love you." Jonathan's breath was warm against her ear.

She stopped walking as her brain tried to process what he'd just said. She stared up at him with her lips parted.

Jonathan wasn't looking at her. Instead, he was focused on Rob, who stood at the end of the aisle.

What did he just say?

"Jonathan..." was all she could muster before he turned back to her and smiled.

"It's okay. I just wanted you to know. I wanted to say those words out loud and for you to hear them." He unhooked their arms and moved his hand until it rested on the small of her back. "But we are really holding up the line."

Tiffany glanced behind her to see the earnest expression of Heather, who was nodding for Tiffany to keep moving.

The world around her blurred as she allowed Jonathan to lead her down the aisle. Just as they approached Rob and the pastor, Jonathan smiled down at her as he peeled off to the side to stand behind the other groomsmen.

It took some brain power, but Tiffany finally made it behind Beatrice where she belonged.

Thankfully, all she had to do was stand there while the wedding ceremony took place. Honestly, she wasn't really paying attention to what was going on.

All her thoughts kept returning to Jonathan and his declaration. The fact that he could so openly say those words caused goosebumps to rise on her skin. It was the most glorious thing she'd ever heard, and, at the same time, it was the scariest as well.

His words caused a flurry of emotions to rush through her, causing her to shake.

When the wedding ceremony was finally over and Stacy and Rob walked back down the aisle, Tiffany hesitated before forcing herself to join up with Jonathan.

He smiled down at her as he linked his arm through hers.

They walked in time with the other wedding party members. Jonathan was surprisingly quiet as they neared the exit.

"I don't expect you to say it back," he whispered. "In fact, I'm sure you don't want to. But I need you to know that I'm here. I'm waiting for you." His voice deepened. "When you're ready."

They walked through the atrium's doors and out into the foyer. The desire to flee raced through Tiffany. As if he sensed her reaction, Jonathan wrapped his hand around her elbow and pulled her to the side.

"Tiffany," he said.

All she could do was look up at him.

"I will always be your friend. I will always be here. Even if you turn me down…again, I'll stick around. I'm not going to let you go." He leaned in and pressed his lips to the top of her head. "I'm in it for the long haul."

"Tiffany! Pictures!" Heather squealed as she rushed over to grab Tiffany.

Not sure what to do or say, Tiffany turned to focus on Heather, who was studying her.

"What did you do, Jonathan? You stunned our little Tiffany into silence."

Jonathan just shrugged. "Just spoke the truth." He winked at Heather and then turned to look at Tiffany. He smiled and made his way over to the crowd of groomsmen that were getting ready to head out for pictures as well.

"Everything okay? You look like you've seen a ghost," Heather said as she linked arms with Tiffany and ushered her toward the doors.

Tiffany cleared her throat, finally coming out of the hazy fog she'd been in since Jonathan's declaration. "Yeah. I, um…"

Heather stopped and turned so she was facing Tiffany. "What happened?"

Tiffany pinched her lips together. She wasn't sure she

could actually say the words. But Heather looked so earnest, so Tiffany decided to try whispering them.

"He said he loves me."

Heather balked at her. "He what?"

"He said he loves me."

Heather's eyebrows shot up. "Wow. Well he took the bull by the horns. Nice job."

Tiffany shook her head. "No. Not nice. Shocking. Scary. I have no idea what I'm going to do with that. What does he want from me?"

She followed Heather through the doors and out into the warm air. Thankfully, there was a beautiful flower garden a few feet off, and Tiffany made a beeline for it. She needed to walk.

"Wait up," Heather said, following after her.

Once they were in the seclusion of the garden, Tiffany began to pace back and forth. "Why would he say that? Why would he do it like that?"

Heather studied her. "Maybe because he likes you? Hold that—he *loves* you."

Tiffany nodded, but she felt more confused than ever. "But doesn't he know that it will ruin our friendship? I suck at dating. He'll never speak to me again if I ruin everything."

"Maybe he doesn't see it like that. I mean, not every relationship is doomed. Some actually do go the distance. Maybe that's what he sees for you two."

Tiffany stopped moving so she could stare down at her cousin. "That's ridiculous. Why would he think that?"

Heather sighed, rolling her eyes in an exaggerated movement. "Because he loves you, dummy. I mean, why else would he still be here? It's not like he knows Stacy or Rob. He's here because of you." She collapsed on a cement bench and leaned back on her hands. "You're kind of naive, cousin of mine."

Tiffany shot her a look and then resumed pacing. "What

am I supposed to do now? He told me he'd wait, that he just wanted me to know how he felt."

Heather tapped her chin as if she were trying to dissect what Tiffany had just said. Then she glanced over at Tiffany and smiled. "I know you probably don't want to hear this, but I love Jonathan. I think he's *the* perfect guy for you."

Tiffany groaned as she shook her head. "No. I don't want to hear that."

Heather shrugged. "Someone's got to say it."

Tiffany threw her hands up in the air as she returned to pacing.

"I guess the question to ask is do you love him back?"

Tiffany stopped moving. She glanced behind her at her cousin. It was such a direct question with so many answers.

She wanted to deny it. She wanted to tell Heather that she was crazy. There was no way she could feel that way about her best friend.

But when she parted her lips to speak, nothing came out. She swallowed as tears brimmed her lids. "I think so," she whispered.

Heather cheered as she sprang up from the bench and rushed over to hug Tiffany. When she pulled back, she was grinning. "Then you need to tell him. Jump in with both feet. Don't be scared of what might happen." Heather patted Tiffany's shoulders. "You just might find what you've been looking for all along. A man who will love you for you."

Tiffany chewed her lip. Jump in. That seemed easy enough. But if that was true, why was her stomach in knots? Why was her heart pounding fear through her body?

Heather sighed. "You've got to let that go."

"What?"

Heather pulled away as she pointed her finger toward Tiffany. "What your dad did. Not every guy is going to abandon you. He was a tool, as was your mom. You've got to start believing that you are worth loving. That you have something to offer. If not, you'll let the greatest love you'll ever find pass you by." Heather crossed her arms, tapping her forearm with her finger.

Tiffany wasn't sure she could face her past and just put it behind her. How does a child ever get over being abandoned by their parents? How?

"I know," she whispered as she toed the grass with her shoe. "I just don't know how to."

Heather sighed. "I know. It's hard. But avoiding situations where you are vulnerable isn't the solution. What if you asked Jonathan to go slow? Would that help?"

Tiffany swallowed. "Maybe? I don't know."

Heather moved over and linked arms with her. "Well, take your time. It sounds like Jonathan isn't going anywhere. He'll give you the time you need to heal." Heather squeezed Tiffany's arm. "Just don't do anything that you might regret. Take things slow and see how you feel then."

Tiffany pushed back her tears as she nodded. The last thing she needed was to walk up to the photoshoot with mascara running down her face.

She doubted she had the strength to talk about what was going on. Anyone with half a brain would think she was crazy for not jumping into Jonathan's arms after he proclaimed his love for her. He was the perfect guy.

She was an idiot to hold back, yet she couldn't find the strength to share her feelings. At least, not yet.

Heather helped guide Tiffany from the gardens and over to the large trees that dotted the hotel's landscaping. The photographer was already there, snapping pictures of the wedding party.

Thankfully, Tiffany was too distracted with smiling and shifting her pose to focus on what Jonathan had said. And he didn't bring it up when they had to stand next to each other.

Instead, he just pressed his hand to her lower back when needed and smiled down at her in a soft and encouraging way.

It made her heart swell each time. Perhaps she could do this. Allow herself, a little at a time, to break down this protective wall she'd put up around her heart and let him in. That thought made her feel lighter than she'd felt in a long time.

By the time they were done, the wedding planner announced that it was time for the reception. Tiffany nodded and kept step with Heather as they made their way into the dining hall.

"Hey, Jonathan," Heather said.

Tiffany glanced over to see that Jonathan had made his way up to them. Her cheeks heated as she met his gaze, and his smile deepened.

"Hey, ladies," he said as he shoved his hands into his pockets. "I was wondering if you guys might save a dance for me."

Tiffany parted her lips, not sure if that was a good idea, but Heather beat her to it.

"Of course, we'd love to."

Jonathan's gaze made its way over to Tiffany and he nodded. "Perfect."

They walked in silence as they headed into the room. Loud music carried from the corner speakers where a DJ was set up. People were already sitting down at the tables or milling around, hugging and talking.

Tiffany slipped over to her table and found her seat. Just as she'd thought, she was sitting next to Jonathan. A few minutes later, he joined her.

He sat down and situated his chair so that he was sitting inches from her. Tiffany was highly aware of how close his elbow was. If she wanted to, it would only take a slight twitch, and her arm would be pressed up against his.

And she'd be lying if she said that wasn't exactly what she wanted to do.

She swallowed down the lump that had formed in her throat and clasped her hands in her lap. That was the last thing she needed. To confuse herself. She needed to keep a level head if she was going to get through the rest of this wedding.

"It was a really beautiful wedding ceremony," Jonathan said, glancing over at her.

Tiffany nodded. It really was. "Yeah. Stacy knows how to throw a party."

Jonathan smiled as he glanced around. Thankfully, a waiter showed up with a tray of champagne flutes. Tiffany took one and sipped on it. She needed the distraction it gave her.

It was so strange to be in this situation. How she could go from feeling completely at ease and comfortable with her best friend to not knowing what to say around him and worrying what he'd think if she said the wrong thing.

How could a relationship go backwards like this?

She didn't like this. At all.

Desperate to fix what was happening, she turned and smiled at him. "Thanks for coming here with me."

Jonathan glanced over at her. "Really? That's how you feel?"

Tiffany furrowed her brow as she nodded. Why would he ask that?

"Good. 'Cause I was worried I'd ruined everything."

Tiffany shook her head. "You didn't ruin everything," she whispered.

He raised his eyebrows. "Are you sure? 'Cause I haven't been able to get you to say more than three words to me since…" His voice trailed off as his gaze flicked down to her lips.

Tiffany's heart pounded. "I know. Things will get better, I promise."

Jonathan met her gaze and smiled. "I know they will. It's just hard. I miss you."

Tiffany blinked, but before she could say anything, the waiter appeared with their plates of food. The next twenty minutes were filled with eating, which Tiffany was grateful for.

She needed some time to figure out where she wanted to go from here. She needed to decide if she was going to push forward and accept Jonathan into her heart, or leave. But this back and forth wasn't good for either of them. She was scared, but she needed to face that fear or she was going to lose the only person she'd ever cared about—the only person who cared about her enough to stick around.

After dinner and the couple's first dance, Tiffany glanced over at Jonathan and nodded toward the dance floor.

"Want to?" she asked as a slow '90s ballad picked up.

Jonathan quirked an eyebrow. "You sure?"

Tiffany nodded. "Yep."

Jonathan pushed out his chair and held his hand out for her. "Definitely."

Tiffany took a deep breath and slipped her hand into his. He led her onto the dance floor with one hand pressed lightly to the small of her back. It sent shivers up and down her skin.

She was nervous and scared, but at the same time, she'd never felt safer. Here was a guy who, no matter how much she pulled away, stayed.

He loved her despite how crazy she'd been acting these last few days. He'd proved to her that he wasn't going to hurt her, and she needed to trust that.

Jonathan lifted one hand and wrapped the other around

her waist as he pulled her in. He kept his distance, never pressing her next to him. Which made her sad.

Glancing up, she found him staring at her with a soft, yet intense, expression.

"Is this okay?" he asked as he knit his eyebrows together.

Tiffany nodded. "Yes."

"Good."

They danced in silence, and Tiffany wanted to break it. She wanted to be brave and speak the words that were on the tip of her tongue. She wanted to let him know how she felt.

She'd been so confused by her feelings and what they meant, but now, none of that seemed to matter. Jonathan was still here. At a wedding for someone he didn't know.

All for her.

She sucked in her breath and looked up at him. "I'm sorry," she whispered.

He glanced down at her. "For what?"

"For running. For pushing you away. For not being strong enough for you." A tear escaped her eye, and she swallowed, hoping to gather the courage she was sorely lacking.

Jonathan shook his head. "It's okay. I understand. You've been hurt before, and you're worried that I'll hurt you too." His hand tightened against her back as if he wanted her to feel the weight of his words. "But I could never hurt you." He pulled her closer and bent his head down until their cheeks were next to each other. "You're my Leia." Then he pulled back with his nose wrinkled. "But can I be your Hans? If I'm Luke, we'd be related."

Tiffany pinched her lips together to stifle a laugh. It was in vain though. The giggles escaped, and, for the first time in a while, the pain she was feeling escaped with the sound. "Sure."

His eyebrows went up and a hopeful look crossed his face. "Really?"

Tiffany's gaze grew hazy as she studied him. "Yes." Then she pushed up onto her tiptoes and brushed her lips against his. Tingles erupted across her skin and spread down to her toes.

None of the relationships she'd been in had ever felt so completely real as her relationship with Jonathan. He was everything she'd ever wanted in a best friend and in a person to love.

He was perfect for her. They were two puzzle pieces that were meant to fit together.

Jonathan pulled back with a questioning look on his face. "Tiffany, I don't—"

Tiffany reached up and pressed her finger against his lips. "I'm not scared." Then she shook her head. "That's not true. I'm terrified. But I'd rather be terrified with you than be with anyone else." She pressed her hand against his heart. "You are mine. And I'm yours. It's as simple as that. And no matter how much I fight it, I'll still come back to this conclusion."

Jonathan's gaze met hers, and suddenly, he wrapped his arms around her waist and pulled her up to him. He pressed his lips to hers. She could feel everything he wanted to say in that kiss.

Then he pulled back. She giggled as he spun her around on the dance floor. A few disgruntled people murmured under their breath as they had to jump to the side to avoid getting kicked.

Jonathan set her down, apologized, and then grabbed her hand and pulled her off the dance floor.

CHAPTER SEVENTEEN

Jonathan's heart was pounding so hard he was sure that everyone could hear it as he grabbed Tiffany's hand and pulled her from the dance floor. The sound of her laughter caused his heart to soar.

It was hard to believe that he was so lucky as to fall in love with his best friend and to have her love him back.

Once they got outside, he turned and pulled her close to him. He reached up and cradled her cheek in his hand. Her laughter died down as she held his gaze.

Jonathan ran his thumb over her lips as he allowed his feelings to crash over him. He'd been looking for this exact girl all his life just to find out she'd been next to him the whole time. He just hadn't known it.

"I love you," he whispered, his voice giving way to his emotions.

Tiffany's eyes glistened as she stared at him. "I love you, too."

Her words filled every broken crevice in his soul. They were the words he'd been dying to hear, and now that they were spoken, it seemed too good to be true.

He furrowed his brow as he leaned in and pressed his forehead to hers. "Really?" he asked. He silently cursed himself for asking. He should just accept that she'd said it.

Tiffany pulled back and smiled. "I love you. Do you want to know how to know that it's true?"

He grabbed onto her hand and brought it up to press against his lips. "How?" he asked as he glanced up at her over her fingers.

She leaned in. "Because I didn't just jump in when I felt like it." She smiled at him as he straightened and pulled her closer.

He wrapped his arms around her again and pressed her against him. "Then I'm glad." He leaned in and pressed his lips to hers. Then he pulled back. "Can I ask you a question?" His heart pounded in his chest as the question felt as if it were going to explode from his body.

Tiffany nodded. "Sure."

He studied her, and then, in one swift moment, he was down on one knee. Tiffany gasped as she stared at him.

"What are you doing?" Her cheeks flushed as her voice dropped to a whisper.

"Making sure you never go anywhere." He held up her hand. "Tiffany. Will you marry me?"

When she didn't answer right away, Jonathan glanced up, worried he'd done the wrong thing. But when he saw the tears in her eyes, his heart swelled.

"Really?" she asked.

Jonathan wanted to shout his love for her from the rooftops. He wanted to tell everyone just how perfect she was for him. "Yes. Of course. You are my soulmate. My everything." He gently kissed her hand. "Please be Mrs. Jonathan Braxton."

Tiffany studied him, and slowly she began to nod. "Of course."

His heart galloped in his chest. He raised his eyebrows. "Is that a yes?"

Tiffany reached out and tugged on his arm. Jonathan stood. Tiffany pushed up onto her tiptoes and wrapped both arms around his neck.

Jonathan grabbed her waist and pulled her up, crushing his lips against hers.

They stood there, kissing for what felt like an eternity. The world around him faded away as he allowed himself to get lost in her touch. She was everything he was ever going to need.

She was perfect.

He groaned when she pulled back. Her lips were puffy and her expression hazy. She smiled at him as she nodded.

"That's a yes."

Jonathan spun her around, reveling in the sound of her laughter and the curves of her neck as she threw her head back.

She was his. For now and forever. And he'd live his whole life to show her how much he loved her.

Once her laughter died down, Jonathan helped her back down onto the ground, but he kept his arms around her. Realization dawned on him as he started to chuckle.

"You do know what this means, don't you?"

Tiffany snuggled into his chest. "What?"

"We have to tell my mom."

The next day, Jonathan pulled open the back door and stepped into the Braxton kitchen. He and Tiffany had just returned from the wedding. No one knew about their engagement, but that was about to change.

"Who's home?" Sondra's voice carried from the dining room, followed shortly by Jonathan's mom.

"Hey, sweetie, you're back early," she said as she folded her arms and smiled up at him.

"Yeah. We decided to head out as soon as the bride and groom left."

The door slammed behind him and Jonathan turned to see Tiffany behind him. He fought the urge to reach out and thread his fingers through hers.

Thankfully, Sondra didn't seem to notice. Instead, she walked over to the kettle and began to fill it up. "I'll make you two some tea."

"Thanks, Mrs. Braxton," Tiffany said as she walked past him, winking as she went.

Jonathan shot her a look and then glanced over at his mom, who didn't seem to notice their interaction.

"How was the wedding?" Sondra asked, glancing over at Tiffany.

A soft smile spread across Tiffany's lips. "It was…beautiful. Life changing, really."

Sondra studied her and then sighed, directing it mainly to Jonathan. "I wish I could have been there. It's been so long since there's been a wedding in our family." She eyed Jonathan. "Maybe you can help me get one of my boys married," she said as she smiled at Tiffany.

Tiffany giggled just as Jonathan said, "*Ma*."

Sondra shrugged. "I'm ready. I'm not sure what you're waiting for."

Jonathan shook his head. And then he walked over and wrapped his arms around Sondra's shoulders. He dipped down to her ear and whispered, "Tiffany is already helping me."

Sondra stiffened and there was a long pause before she whipped around, screeching as she went.

"What?" Then she stuck her finger into Jonathan's chest. "Don't be playing with me, child. I brought you into this world, and I can take you out."

Jonathan held up his hands just as his dad walked into the kitchen.

"What are you screaming about?"

Sondra wiped her hands on her apron. "Your son here is mean. He's playing with my poor heart."

"I'm—"

"Why are you teasing your mom?" Jimmy asked as he grabbed a cookie and leaned against the counter.

"Hey, now. I'm not teasing her." Jonathan walked over to Tiffany and held out his hand. Tiffany took it and entwined her fingers with his as she stood up. "We're engaged."

Jimmy must have inhaled cookie crumbs because he began coughing. Sondra had tears streaming down her cheeks as she reached out and began whacking Jimmy on the back. They were definitely a sight to see.

The back door opened and Josh stepped in. He looked around the room, incredibly confused.

Jonathan pointed at Tiffany. "We're engaged."

"Makes sense." Then he crossed the kitchen and reached out his hand. "Congrats you two."

Tiffany wrapped her arms around Jonathan's stomach and smiled. "Thanks."

Thankfully, his parents regained their composure and were soon over to the two of them, wrapping them in a huge hug. Sondra was crying and listing off everyone she needed to call. Jimmy was just clearing his throat and welcoming Tiffany to the clan o' Braxton.

Suddenly, a phone was shoved into Jonathan's hand. His mom was staring up at him with an eager look. "Call your brothers. Maybe you'll inspire them."

Jonathan groaned, but his mom gave him her no-

nonsense look. Sighing he took it. "I'll do it, Mom, but I doubt it will have the effect you think it will."

Sondra shrugged. "At this point, I'll do just about anything."

Taking a moment to kiss Tiffany, Jonathan leaned in and pressed his lips to hers. She giggled as she patted his chest. "Go. I doubt your mom will leave you alone until you do."

Groaning, Jonathan tipped his forehead down to touch hers. "Love you."

She nodded. "Love you."

EPILOGUE

James

The low hum of chatter dulled James's senses as he sat in the far booth at Piston's Bar. The dark light and secluded table helped him feel safe—something that was a constant struggle for him now, after…

Clearing his throat, James reached out and grabbed the glass of whisky. He muscled down his memories as if that was the answer to dealing with his past.

He could almost hear his therapist, Dr. Georgina, as she repeated the words she said during every one of his sessions.

"You need to face your past. Running from it will only ensure that it stays with you."

James closed his eyes as his frustration at what had happened in his past threatened to bubble over. Dr. Georgina didn't understand. How could she? She hadn't been there. She had no idea what it felt like to be that alone.

"Hey, man."

James opened his eyes to see Juan, his best friend, drop

into the seat across from him. His dark hair was swept to the side, and he looked as if he'd run all the way here.

"You okay?"

Juan shrugged. "Yeah. Just family issues."

The waitress stopped by and Juan ordered a pint. Once she was gone, James straightened in his seat, grateful for the distraction his friend's problems were sure to give him.

"Layla?" James asked. Layla was Juan's younger sister, who always seemed to be in the wrong place at the wrong time.

Juan shrugged. "Something like that."

James furrowed his brow as he stared at his friend. What did that mean?

Juan waved away James's questioning gaze as the waitress dropped off his beer. After a long drink, Juan glanced at James. "It's okay. We'll be fine."

James's phone rang. He studied his friend, but from the look in his eye, he really wasn't going to share anything more. So he shifted and grabbed his phone from his pocket.

It was Jonathan.

"It's my brother," he said, holding his phone up. Juan nodded as James brought the receiver to his ear.

"Hey," he said.

"James?"

"Yeah."

"It's Jonathan."

"I know."

"Tell him." James could hear his mother's pushy voice on the other end of the call.

"Hey, Ma," he said as he fought the urge to smile. His mom was nosy, but she loved her kids.

"Hey, James," Sondra called, the sound of her voice growing louder as she got closer to the phone.

"Can I talk to him now?" Jonathan asked.

Sondra muttered something as her voice grew fainter.

"Sorry. You know Mom," Jonathan said.

James nodded. "She doesn't change." He cleared his throat. "What's up?"

Jonathan paused. "I'm getting married."

James furrowed his brow. "You're what?"

"I'm getting married!"

"To who?"

"What do you mean, to who? To Tiffany."

James sat back, leaning against the booth. "Congrats, man. That's amazing."

"And I want you to be my best man."

James reached out and drummed his fingers on the tabletop. "Sure. Of course. I'd be honored."

He could hear Jonathan blow out a breath on the other side. "Perfect. We're planning it now. You're coming here, right?"

It wasn't like he had much else to do, so James said, "I'll pencil you in."

"Perfect. I'll call you later with more details."

"Yep." James couldn't help the smile that formed on his lips. "Hey, Jonathan?"

"Yeah?"

"Congrats. I'm really happy for you."

"Thanks. Talk to you later?"

"Yep."

They said their goodbyes and James hung up. He slipped his phone back into his pocket and glanced up at Juan, who was studying him.

"Which brother was that?"

"Jonathan. He's getting married."

Juan nodded. "Wow. That's exciting."

"Yeah."

The table grew quiet as they sat there. James cleared his

throat and shoved his hands through his hair. "I'm happy for him, you know? He deserves to find that one girl to spend his life with." When he met Juan's gaze, he couldn't help but feel as if his best friend was studying him.

James sighed. "What?"

Juan shook his head. "Nothing." Then he leaned forward. "Maybe it'll inspire some people."

James snorted as he shook his head. He knew what Juan was getting at. "Yeah. Not all of us are blessed with finding the perfect girl." He nodded toward the ring on Juan's left hand.

Juan leaned back in the booth and shrugged. "She's out there for you, man. You just need to be more open to letting it in."

James swallowed as he emptied his drink. He wanted to say that Juan was right. That he still believed in fate, but the truth was he didn't.

Happiness just wasn't in the cards for him, and he needed to accept that. Besides, no woman wanted a broken man. And he was pretty sure he couldn't be pieced back together.

Not by Dr. Georgina, and definitely not by some woman.

James Braxton was meant to live alone. Forever.

***

Join my Newsletter!
Find great deals on my books and other sweet romance!
Get, Fighting Love for the Cowboy FREE
just for signing up!
Grab it HERE!

SHE'S AN IRS AUDITOR DESPERATE TO PROVE HERSELF.
HE'S A COWBOY TRYING TO HOLD ONTO HIS RANCH.
LOVE WAS NOT ON THE AGENDA.

OTHER BOOKS BY ANNE-MARIE MEYER

Clean Adult Romances

Forgetting the Billionaire

Book 1 of the Clean Billionaire Romance series

Second Chance Mistletoe Kisses

Book 1 of Love Tries Again series

Second Chance at Christmas Inn

Book 3 of Love Tries Again Series

Coming Home to Honey Grove

Book 1 of A Braxton Family Romance series

Friendship Blooms in Honey Grove

Book 2 of A Braxton Family Romance series

Escaping to Honey Grove

Book 3 of A Braxton Family Romance series

Forgiveness Found in Honey Grove

Book 4 of A Braxton Family Romance series

Christmas in Honey Grove

Book 5 of A Braxton Family Romance series

Her Second Chance

Book 0 of the Braxton Brothers series

Fighting Love for the Cowboy

Book 1 of A Moose Falls Romance

ABOUT THE AUTHOR

Anne-Marie Meyer lives in MN with her husband, four boys, and baby girl. She loves romantic movies and believes that there is a FRIENDS quote for just about every aspect of life.

Connect with Anne-Marie on these platforms!
anne-mariemeyer.com

Made in the USA
Monee, IL
09 March 2021